IT CAME FROM SPACE IV
THE GATHERING

EDDIE GENEROUS

SEVERED PRESS

IT CAME FROM SPACE IV

1

Denver Jones stared at the formerly white cotton wrapped around the nub of his right ankle. It had gone pink, so similar to cotton candy that he laughed until he cried. The pain meds were good and getting away alive was better. The doctor had left him in the back of the SUV to get drinks and snacks. Everyone had departed so quickly and frantically that most minds had bypassed the physical needs. Getting onto the ferry was hurry, hurry, hurry up, while crossing to the mainland was wait, wait, wait.

The windows were down in the SUV and an occasional spray of water found his scalp, cheek, or neck. He couldn't say if it was the rain or the ocean, and was only considering it because what else was there to think about while he floated, both physically and mentally?

His future? His one-footed future?

No, he wasn't ready to think about that just yet.

The vehicles had been crammed onto the ferry and many of the passengers were ignoring the rules concerning staying on the below decks while sailing. Likely everything was packed tight as a can of tuna in the passenger deck as well. As the parking lines had been ignored, opening doors bumped the closed doors of neighboring vehicles all around him. Denver watched a woman do a full spin to see if anyone saw her slam her Aerostar door into the side of a brand-new BMW. Apparently only Denver had because she shuffled away unbothered.

The sounds of the ocean mingled with the coming and going voices of the moving passengers. Gusts of sea-salty air brought the words into the SUV in bursts. Denver wasn't satisfied with that and began shimmying himself toward the interior hatch handle. He'd stained the rug with blood and wondered if he'd owe the doctor something for his service, wondered how to broach the subject. Was this like a house call? Would he be billed? He knew that Canadian taxes ensured residents didn't need to foot the bill themselves, but what about American guests? Like him.

He got the rear hatch open and felt the fresh whoosh of oceanic atmosphere. From where he sat, he could look out at all the vehicles that had gotten on after the SUV that had brought him. It made him think of Christmas shopping, or how it had been before Amazon simplified the task online. As a boy, his mother would take him to the Woodbine Mall ten minutes from home. She'd give him sixty bucks and with that cash he had to pick out gifts for her, his father, and the family dog, adding that he had to meet her at the McDonald's in the food court no later than three, or four, or whatever was two hours after they'd arrived. Denver would run, frantic and clueless on what to get anyone but the dog, Chubbs. Chubbs was easy and those big, greasy bones were only about eight bucks back then. But his father, Dale, and his mother, Cynthia, they were impossible. Almost always it was a checkered button-up shirt for him and a small jug of perfume—that she'd never wear after testing it Christmas morning—and a box of chocolates, which they'd all partake in eating.

Denver felt his pants pocket for his cellphone with the sudden urge to call his mother. The feeling of thankfulness invaded in such a way that it was tough not to cry. He could be dead, and dead boys don't get to say goodbye to their mothers one last time. The phone had fallen out of his pocket but was there next to him on the damp and matted carpet.

No bars. Of course not. He'd need a satellite phone out here.

"Hey," the doctor said. He was a short man named Goldstein—likely he had a given name as well, but he hadn't said it in Denver's presence. "They weren't giving options on food. Just these shrink-wrapped monstrosities." He held up a coffee cup and a cellophaned piece of lemon loaf with a half-inch of white icing on top.

Denver winced as he reached to take the cup and the snack.

"I have cream and sugar in my pocket, if you need them," Goldstein said.

"Don't think it'll matter. My mouth tastes like I've been sucking a battery."

Goldstein nodded and smiled. "I knew this kid called Jerry who used to suck coin batteries and chew tinfoil. He never graduated college, but his father bought him a car wash, which turned a profit and allowed him to buy a couple laundromats. I figured he'd be haunting a fourth floor somewhere for the entirety of his adulthood. Shows you never know about a guy."

Denver moved to set down his coffee and the boat rocked heavily. He spilled a quarter of the cup on his hand. He hissed beneath his breath but got the cup safely settled so he could tackle the wrapper on the lemon loaf. He took a mouthful of uber-sweet bread that had his salivary glands working overtime, the sugar instantly dancing in his veins, so thickly that he could feel it everywhere.

"It will take some time to learn to live with only one foot," Goldstein said after he sat down on a clean spot of the carpet, next to Denver's nub. "I think you'll come to feel fortunate, especially if you should meet other amputees, those missing more of themselves."

Denver tried to swallow but the mouthful refused to go down. He drowned it with coffee.

"I've known children who have grown into adulthood, fully adjusted—that's my field, I'm in pediatrics—missing a seemingly vital part."

Denver got the mouthful down and said, "You don't happen to have a satellite phone, do you?"

Goldstein grinned widely as he straightened his back. "As a matter of fact, I do. For some reason, I assumed Picture Island to be less inhabited. I went out and got a waterproof case—phone's already water resistant, but…you know, better safe than sorry." He shoveled home the last of his own sugary loaf and washed it away, wincing as he did so, with his light brown coffee. "It's in the glovebox." Goldstein pushed the swinging hatch door closed enough to pass and went to the front.

2

Jacy Popper quit dragging the barely conscious George McNaughton and ran to the check-in desk for the wheeled computer chair while Lin Hubbard locked the doors behind them. The enormous cougar had seemed to lose interest in them beyond the paranoia of whatever drew its attention away in the first place. The doors were glass and could hardly pose much safety in the face of such a situation, so it was good that Jacy had at least a piece of a plan in suggesting they go to the kitchen.

"Help me," Jacy said, hands on George's left arm.

"Why the kitchen?" Lin said, taking George's right side.

They got him into the chair handily and Jacy began to push through the dining area. The hotel was quiet, and that only seemed to magnify the loudness of the enormous beasts beyond the building.

"Food…and better walls," Jacy said, the second half coming as if she'd only just considered it; having food was a top priority for the short-term.

They reached the kitchen, and the deep-fryer scent was thick and welcoming. The grill, fridge, and freezer all hummed enough to drown out the otherworldliness outside. Once the wheels of the computer chair humped over the lip where the dining room rug met kitchen tile, the scary noises were completely lost to the mundane.

"Do you want fries? Chicken fingers?" Jacy said.

Mandy Ng, her boss, let her eat all the fries she wanted on her work shifts—probably because she paid so far below minimum wage, partly why anyway—and now and then she snuck a chicken finger into the basket. She guessed if she'd asked, Mandy would've been okay with it, but if she wasn't, she couldn't do it at all. Better to sneak and apologize if she got caught. Though, now, it hardly seemed like it was going to matter. Picture Island was turning into a Canadian *Jurassic Park*.

"Yes," George whispered. He looked at Lin. "You got down."

"That I did," Lin said.

George closed his eyes, barely remaining upright on the chair.

Jacy was in the freezer with a fryer basket, loading up chicken fingers and fries. "Ooh, mozza sticks. I love those. And jalapeno poppers. My dad always jokes about how we should be rich since they're probably a family tradition or something. Like from our ancestors. But I know he's only joking. Mandy doesn't have any poppers, but do you want mozza sticks?" She looked over her shoulder to Lin who had hopped up to sit on the chopping board prep counter, her right knee folded over her left to pick at the sticky web still clinging.

"Yeah, sure," Lin said.

"What do you want to drink? Should I get George whiskey? Sometimes my grandma would give all the kids whiskey if we were sick, before bed I mean. Is it whiskey they put on dogs to give to lost skiers? I think those dogs are super smart," Jacy said. Thoughtlessly, she'd tossed the chicken fingers and mozza sticks into the same fryer basket. The mozza sticks were almost halfway done in seconds while the chicken fingers would take the longest, a handful of minutes even.

"I'd take a beer… No whiskey for you kids, and no, that's brandy, and that dogs carried casks on their necks is a myth. I agree dogs are super smart; some dogs." Lin pushed down to her feet. "I'll get the drinks from the bar. What do you want?"

"Since we're breaking Mandy's rules, can you get me some chocolate milk? She only lets me have water and fountain pop, but I don't think anything matters anymore. This town is done for," Jacy said.

"Ginger ale…I don't feel too good," George said and then began sliding, the chair shooting out behind him as he dropped slowly to the floor.

"Got linens in here?" Lin said and Jacy nodded. "Make him a nest on the counter and we'll get him off the floor."

"The mozza sticks are ready," Jacy said.

"So take them out," Lin said, starting away.

"The chicken fingers are with them, so I have to do this first or you do it and I build the nest!" Jacy shouted.

Lin didn't answer. Jacy got to snatching at the floating brown sticks and popping them into a steel bowl typically used to sauce wings. Once they were out, she dropped the tongs and they clattered across the counter and into the sink with a clang. She then ran to the linen closet on the far side of the kitchen and swung open the double doors. She grabbed all the table cloths she could handle and hurried back to the cutting board island in the middle of the kitchen.

While Jacy was busy at this, Lin hurried back through the kitchen door. She had a liter jug of chocolate milk dangling from a finger, three cans of Heineken on a plastic ring, a tall glass of ginger ale, and an unopened pack of Player's Light cigarettes between her teeth. She set the drinks down next to the nest fixins and turned back to the door. There was a broom leaned against the door frame and she jammed the wooden shaft through the steel door handle. The bottom of the broom nestled in behind the legs of the industrial dishwasher.

She pulled the cigarette pack from her mouth and said, "There's a fly out there as big as a football."

Jacy nodded. "Mozza sticks are ready." She stood on her tippy toes to get a better angle into the fryer basket from where she stood. "So are the fries. Is that enough for George?" Jacy pointed to the linens she'd gathered.

Lin nodded. "Tend to our food and I'll fix his bed. I have kids, I've done this before."

Jacy pulled the fry basket out and let it drain. She shook the chicken finger basket. They weren't brown enough yet. "Good thing you didn't die. George's parents are dead and so is his grandma and the guy who was going to be his dad killed himself too. My parents are stuck on a cruise ship. Quarantined."

"I can't imagine taking a cruise these days," Lin said.

"It was real cheap," Jacy said as she fixed three

heaping plates. "I can't imagine getting stuck in a spider web…or maybe I can. Yeah, I can. I just said that."

Together they lifted George up onto the makeshift nest. He'd been awake the entire time.

3

Chuck O'Shea had been in the Canadian Navy for twelve years before retiring from service and taking up residence in Ghost Clearing. The last twenty years, he'd worked as a roofer, and only part-time for the last few. After the gator had torn the town to bits, he'd worked nearly two weeks full-time before giving the boss his notice, effective immediately.

"My man," he'd said, "I can't do it anymore. I can't so much as lift another shingle."

To Chuck's surprise, the boss smiled and nodded. "Who had day thirteen?"

After seeing the destruction, resulting workload, and understaffing thanks to losing a couple guys to fairly severe injuries sustained while fleeing the Picture House Lodge most of the way through *The Thing*, getting a team together wasn't easy. But that did not change the men in the crew, or how they passed the mindless hours of hard labor.

"Somebody had thirteen?" the boss said.

The men laughed among themselves.

Chuck had been threatening to retire for the last two years, taking on fewer hours as the months passed. There was no retirement package from roofing—he already received a steady, though slim, income from his service pension—but he'd filed the forms online to start taking his citizen pension. Being sixty-six, he was due.

"Wouldn't it be something to retire and die the next week," he had said to himself as he opened the bunker door to let some air in.

He'd gotten into the lodge after speaking with Mandy, only to find the fuse panel attached to the hidden basement bunker and the air raid siren to be useless. A rat or something had gotten in and chewed the wires, and it didn't look like it had happened recently. Being a man of his age and life experience, he only had to sigh. He hurried home for his toolbelt—reloaded it with items befitting electrical work—and drove to the variety, grocery, and hardware store. The ferry was just loading up then, the rain really starting to come down.

The store was unlocked but vacated. He went to the back and grabbed the heavy-gauge wire and two dusty boxes of glass fuse bulbs that had probably been there since the Toronto Maple Leafs last hoisted the Stanley Cup. He didn't bother leaving money or a note and hurried back out to his truck. The town was done, no arguing that one now. He paused a moment and decided he'd better grab some fresh groceries in case the need to hunker down came into play.

He loaded two bags of high-calorie snack foods, two five-gallon jugs of water, and a case of Kokanee beer into the truck. Within minutes, he had replaced the two visibly destroyed wires to the fuse panel and swapped in the new fuses. He cranked the air raid siren—it would make plenty of noise without the sound system running off the fuse panel, but not nearly enough. As he did so, he thought about lugging the groceries down and taking a nap. He refused to let himself think about the huge animals because those thoughts inevitably led to his thinking about his funeral and the life he'd maybe wasted working so hard.

When he quit turning the siren crank, the noise tapered off like the flapping nozzle of a deflating balloon. Probably wasn't smart to sound it too much, he might draw unwanted attention rather than get the locals still stuck on the island to a safe place.

He stood with his hand on the crank, paused, thinking he'd come back to the siren in an hour or so, when in the absence of his making heaps of noise, he heard a chittering coming from behind him. He spun and a raccoon the size of a black bear scurried out of the shadowy hallway that led to the hall's tiny kitchen.

"Look at you!" Chuck said.

He snatched up his Estwing hammer from the hook of his toolbelt and cocked it behind his head. The raccoon paused a moment, though was not looking at Chuck. Chuck glanced to his right, and in the lodge's foyer was a river otter, nearly as big as the raccoon. The otter hissed once, forced out an especially stinking spray of green shit, and then crouched. The trio stood still then, eyes darting back and forth. A minute passed. Two. Chuck's head began to swim and as he let out a pent breath, it whistled between his lips, and he sucked it back. The creatures still didn't move. Chuck didn't move, though he was so tense he thought he might begin to laugh.

During his service, he'd never seen any combat, but once, he'd been in a silent, moveless standoff:

Canadian submarine against a Russian submarine. It took a while, but the Russians eventually acknowledged they were indeed beyond their waters. They turned back with a warning and air seemed to let out of the *room*. Chuck had laughed then. In all his life he hadn't been so pumped up with adrenaline and fear.

That very feeling was upon him now.

He exhaled the rest of his pent air before sucking deeply. The creatures looked at him and then one another and then him again. He puckered his lips, fighting off a deranged cackle, and began to whistle the standoff tune from *The Good, the Bad, and the Ugly*. The beasts took this as an invitation to step closer; not wanting to look like a weak link, Chuck did the same. He whistled the tune again. As if planned, the moment after he concluded, the trio each drew a step closer. If a boxing ring had been plopped into the room, they'd all be at a corner.

The otter hissed and sprayed out another foul-smelling shit. Chuck turned his head slightly, grimacing at the full-bodied aroma. He'd been walking a trail in the national park once, near a large pond, and a pair of silky little otters had come out of the creek to hiss him away, dropping those same sticking kinds of plops along the path. That shit had smelled a special kind of offensive then and it was spectacularly offensive now.

Particularly to the raccoon.

It leapt, claws outstretched. Chuck leaned away. The otter slipped along the floor like an eel. The raccoon pounced and the otter bit its leg. Chuck made a snap decision. If it came down to two of them, he didn't think he'd catch the otter with his hammer, it was simply too fast. The otter was chewing and squealing as the raccoon thrashed its back, carving divots in its flesh. Chuck spun the hammer in his grip and swung. The claw side slammed down into the otter's head and the raccoon stumbled back, holding its leg in an eerily human manner. The blood trail was slick and thick, shining blackly beneath the bug-dirty fluorescents. The raccoon began whining, still stumbling in reverse, dragging the hurt leg. Chuck freed his hammer and spun it again. He slammed it down five more times for good measure.

The raccoon watched him from where it had come to a stop against a wall. Chuck straightened. Blood had splashed up the legs of his Levi's jeans and had painted his forearms and hands. He cocked the hammer back behind his head, blood dripping down onto his shoulder.

"Well, my man," he said and stalked toward the injured creature.

4

Mandy watched through the ground-level window. The rain slashed the blade of an eastern wind, coming so heavily that the giant cougar had gone off for cover and that the trio of massive moose huddled together in the semi-shade of some high, high spruce trees. The air raid siren had been quiet for about ten minutes. The last boats that had taken people out to sea were now specks in the distance—the ferry would've been clear enough, should any of them care to climb out of the basement to get a better angle. No matter what, she'd be waiting at least four hours until it was again docked at Picture Island.

"If it even comes back," she mumbled to herself.

Bunched up against the southern wall, equal parts away from the window and the open western end were ten locals. They were huddled as if for protection or perhaps play-making. Once in a while, a representative of them would veer away from the wall to listen in on the conversation between the real estate agent and the mercenary before hurrying back with news.

Mandy blinked at them, shaking her head gently. She'd never noticed how weird the locals were. At least the ones left. She wished Garth and James were still around. They'd already be acting, getting them to safety somehow. But they were dead, blown to bits with the fucking space gator that had somehow caused this ongoing mess.

Richard Tomlinson started out from the group and announced to Mandy, "We're going to hide in the terminal. There's running water and food." The food came in the form of two snack machines.

"Okay?" Mandy said.

Dillon, Richter Cohagen's hired muscle, was talking to Miriam Weever about properties while they looked at a map on Dillon's tablet. Both glanced at Richard before turning back to the information.

"Are all of you on Facebook?" Miriam said.

Ten heads nodded, almost in unison.

Miriam's eyes returned to the tablet and what Dillon was whispering. The ten-some shifted their collective attention to Mandy. Richard said, "Want to come with us?"

"Nah," Mandy said. She didn't see the need to point out that a building with a wall more than halfway made of glass was not a safe place, no matter the amenities.

Richard nodded at Mandy and then stepped past her, climbing onto the bench to pull himself out the window. The stairwell that led to the now destroyed shed had a treacherous looking amount of debris littering its steps. Mandy helped to push an elderly woman the last six inches through the window. She watched them cut across the parking lot, running bent over like sniper fire might come at any moment. They made it completely uncontested.

The basement had become quiet, all the noise coming from beyond. Mandy watched for animal activity, hoping everyone still stuck in Ghost

Clearing was hunkered down and safe.

Miriam patted Dillon's muscled left bicep and started toward Mandy where she stood on the bench beneath the window, long rifle in her grip.

"Dillon doesn't think this is a great place either."

Mandy glanced behind her. She was short enough that standing on the bench only gave her a couple inches on Miriam. "Nor do I. So, where's he want us to go?"

Miriam shrugged. "The bunker, I guess, but first, do you know where the town records are kept?"

Mandy nodded. "They're in the old library. Might've closed too long ago for you to know about. There's no basement under where the council meets so they file everything in the old library. That happens to be beneath a rental house. Probably some looky-loo had it rented and hitched a ride out on the boat, I suspect."

"Do you know the address?"

Mandy did but said, "No, I can take you, but after we have to swing by the hotel. Jacy and George ran in there. I'm almost certain it was them."

"What do you say?" Miriam said, half-turned to speak to Dillon.

"The faster the better. This really isn't much of a place for civilians right now," he said.

Mandy snorted a laugh. This was the first remotely humane thing the man had said. He was a robot, just like every mercenary she'd ever seen on TV. Nothing mattered to guys like him but doing the job. He'd likely seen too many deaths to put value on lives not attached to his paycheck.

"Faster the better to get the paperwork done?" Mandy said.

Miriam shrugged when she made eye-contact with Mandy.

The tablet sounded the alert of an incoming call. Dillon held it up like a shaving mirror. "What's the word?"

"Boss wants me to escort you two to the bunker after securing the necessary paperwork that cannot be obtained online," Dillon said.

"Fine by me," Mandy said. "As long as we check in on the hotel."

"First we wait on Scotty." Dillon slipped the tablet into a cargo pocket on his leg.

"First we wait on Scotty, huh?" Mandy said.

Miriam put on her best saleswoman smile.

5

The boat was too small to offer cover to even a third of the people standing onboard. Lucy Weight squinted against the steady slashing rain and the wind that seemed to come from every direction. She couldn't see her store front from where she was, but she saw the biggest moose stomping down the block, its head rising above a few of the buildings— the ones without apartments over business space. Its rack only left sight when the thing bent down.

She'd only just finished putting out a fresh helping of stock—and had triple that to put out, by and by. This fact had her feeling sorry for herself. Though she'd been safe inside and missed all the super-sized animals and insects face-to-face, she'd heard enough about them to know Picture Island was all but cancelled. Her only hope seemed to be that Miriam wasn't joking when she asked if Lucy wanted to sell and leave the island. It seemed highly unlikely that anyone would be buying now. A town infested with beasts wasn't exactly livable.

"At least you made it off safely," she whispered, shivering against the rain and blowback from the ocean. They were rocking enough that she'd heard several people vomiting and had felt a couple lurches up from her guts herself. She hadn't barfed on a boat in her entire life, though she'd never been out in one in this weather, at least not on a fishing boat. Thankfully, they were puttering along.

"Go! Go faster!" a man shouted from a few feet to Lucy's left, also almost leaning over the stern to point into the water.

Lucy let her eyes follow that finger. They'd made it about three miles offshore, and town was more a set of shapes; an idea through the mist. Between the boat and the island was a whole lot of rocky water. It had looked charcoal under the overcast sky but was darkening by the second…aside from two white, white blobs. Lucy squinted harder, trying to understand what she was looking at.

Someone screamed.

The man from before said, "Faster!"

Two of the burly sailors rushed to the stern and looked out before turning around, shoving their way through the crowded deck.

Lucy watched all this, still not making sense of what was happening. They began to tilt and then seemed to float on air, no longer pushing forward. A second later, she saw the rows of enormous teeth rise up out of the water. They tipped hard and Lucy stumbled forward. Someone grabbed her, but it was too late. Her feet slipped along the wet deck before lifting and dragging the man who'd grabbed her, together, they were the first to fall into the black, black gulley of the massive orca's throat. She landed against something soft and wet. The air was putrid and unbreathable. She gagged and gasped, began retching. She heard distant rifle play and the splash of huge amounts of water. Her brain compared the sound to her dishwasher emptying, only a million times as loudly. A deluge of lunch came up her throat and out her nose and mouth in a hot and chunky stew.

She wasn't sick long, however. The fishing boat followed her and the man who had tried to hold her dropped down, down, down into the whale, and she was crushed against a mound of slowly digesting seals at the base of the whale's guts.

6

Perhaps it was the drugs. Perhaps it was multiple near-death experiences. Perhaps it was a little bit of each—alongside losing a foot—that had him feeling nostalgic and missing his mother so much. She hadn't answered the call when he'd dialed with Dr. Goldstein's satellite phone. He set it next to him on the carpeted floor of the SUV trunk. He looked down to the pink wrapping over his nub and remembered the housecoat his mother had worn from about the time he was eight until he was fourteen. It had been almost the same color.

She'd held him in the housecoat, scolded him in that housecoat, prepared him breakfast and ordered him to open his Christmas presents in that housecoat. Including the telescope she and Denver's father had purchased him one year. He'd looked to the black sky and all the shining balls of gas and all the planets and had wanted to be an astronaut. It shifted with the reality of competition when his downfalls became apparent. Space never left him. He nerded out so, so hard on *Star Trek* and *Battlestar Galactica* as a kid and then as a teen. He'd felt an honest pang of sadness when Pluto was demoted while he was an adult.

Now all this stargazing had him on the brink of death. Of course, a foot was a small price to pay for what he'd experienced. Once he got back, he'd be an all-star, and that foot might even help him.

Eventually people would deny the craziness of Picture Island and a missing foot would make one hell of an argument to prove his experiences.

"Did you see that boat out there?" Goldstein said.

There were gaps in the hull of the ferry walls, barely visible from where they were. Goldstein had a better view of just about everywhere thanks to being on his feet and not stuck inside the cargo hold of a vehicle.

"Where?" Denver said, trying to crane around without bumping his tender nub.

"It was just north of us. Then it disappeared. Hold on a moment, I'd like to look, it had been going our speed so long…" Goldstein trailed and started away, weaving through the parked vehicles.

Denver watched him until it became too much hassle to turn. He guessed he'd be in tremendous pain if it weren't for the drugs, which seemed to have him sinking deeper and deeper into a fuzzy, cotton world with each passing minute. He'd only ever felt this kind of high when he'd gotten an endoscope to explore the root of some pained guts—it had been an ulcer. It wasn't a bad way to feel at all.

He slumped back and gazed distantly out the open rear end of the ferry. There was a single fishing vessel out there. It was a good ways back and just beyond where the ferry's waves would give it trouble. Denver wondered what it was like to be a fisherman. They sometimes found things just as interesting—well, maybe not quite—as deep space exploration. The creatures that dwelled, way, way down, the ones that handled unfathomable amounts of pressure, they sometimes rose up and floated for the fishermen to discover and marvel over.

"Lantern fish," Denver said as his mind floated somewhere beyond the here and now.

Distantly, two rifle blasts echoed, just barely, over the din of the ferry and the active ocean.

"Where'd it go?" someone shouted, dragging Denver from reverie.

People were up and moving, heading toward the back of the ferry like a thrum of Black Friday shoppers. Dr. Goldstein came rushing over to Denver and the SUV. He was wide-eyed and excited, soaked from the pounding rain.

"That boat's gone, and another one behind us just disappeared," he said.

A woman went running toward a steel staircase, and as she passed the SUV, she said, "A giant killer whale got 'em!"

Denver and the doctor looked back and within seconds, a massive spout of water blasted sky-high from the rocky surf.

Absently, the doctor said, "Killer whales got their name from their willingness to attack larger breeds of whales."

Denver looked at him. "I did not know that," he said and grasped the satellite phone, thinking he'd better call his mom again.

As he was about to punch in the numbers, the PA system bing-bonged and then crackled. "This is your captain speaking. Due to unforeseen dangers, I will be throttling up. Things will get rocky. Steer clear of the decks."

"He can't possibly think a whale would attack a ferry," Goldstein said.

Denver, phone in hands, raised numbers unpunched, grinned in manic understanding. "If it has space gator blood in it, I wouldn't count anything out. It's—"

The boat jerked and rocked, sending Denver sideways. His nub flared out painfully and the phone skittered beyond his reach. Goldstein tumbled and slipped to his ass on the wet floor. Others screamed. The boat had to be going twice as fast as it had been, really riding the motion of the ocean.

Denver sat upright and grimaced at the bolt of pain. He scanned around him and immediately flopped to his left side. He crawled, only thought being to get the phone now teetering on the lip of the cargo hold. The pain redoubled with each rock. That phone teetered and tottered, as if teasing him.

"Jesus," Goldstein said, rising and leaning on the bumper of the SUV.

Denver didn't hear him. Reaching, he stretched, stretched, stretched as the phone tipped back and forth, as much out of the cargo hold as in. Sweat streamed from Denver's pores, all over his body now, the agony in his nub was incredible as it rubbed against the carpeted floor.

"Come on!" he said through clenched teeth.

7

Scotty, another mercenary, pulled up in front of the former fish warehouse driving a green Dodge Durango from the late 'nineties. Mandy was the first to climb and shimmy out the window of the ruined fish warehouse basement. Miriam came next, aided by Dillon. Dillon followed swiftly without trouble. He had a massive, square head, and arms like a professional boxer.

"Did you see that?" Mandy said, pointing out to the ocean with her free hand—the other hand, of course, held the barrel of her long rifle.

"See what?" Dillon pulled open the shotgun door of the heavy Dodge.

"That fishing boat disappeared." Mandy had her eyes glued on the rocky waves of the ocean.

"Probably had too many people," Miriam said. She'd gotten into the back seat and was speaking through the open door. She seemed less interested in getting rained on any further than she had been over the idea of drowning locals.

Mandy stared. If that boat had sunk from payload, where were all the people? More importantly, who would go out and get them? She looked to the docks. Sailboats stood out like teeth in a rotten mouth. Everything else was gone, or rather, just about. There was a single, gaudy speedboat. It had absurd flames painted along the hull. In bright yellow, the name VICKY was painted on a fast slant at the bow. If she hooked up a couple of the lifeboats from the backs of the sailboats, then she could get out there and grab anyone stuck floating.

"Look, I need a hand," she said, and started down the pier.

"For what?" Dillon said.

"There might be people drowning out there!" Mandy said, getting frantic over the idea, yelling over her shoulder.

Scotty nodded solemnly. "Okay."

Her assumption was that one of the mercenaries, likely both, could hotwire a simple boat engine, and she wasn't wrong. Miriam helped, reluctantly, forever scanning the shoreline for too big creatures. Inside eight minutes, they had two rowboats tied to the back of the speedboat and the speedboat's engine running. Mandy stood at the helm while the others stood on the dock.

"Please, make sure the kids are okay. I'm sure they're at the hotel. I'd check the kitchen," she called over the rumbling growl of the speedboat's engine.

"Yep!" Miriam said, running to the Dodge.

Mandy began backing up, the rowboats clunking hollowly behind her. This was quite a rescue mission, made doubly unbelievable that neither of those big men offered to join her or take her place. She guessed most mercenaries would watch a child die on an empty street if they weren't hired to save them. The coldness was robotic, though Scotty seemed a hair more human than Dillon.

"What's that matter now?" she said.

She punched the throttle where she crouched

behind the stubby windshield—a mostly pointless chunk of barrier, even at her height. The speed had rocked her back at first, but once she understood the power, she bent her knees in a way that had her upright and boogying. The boat cut the waves with surprising ease, though was not impervious to the thrashing. She could throttle only to about halfway to maximum and even then, had to hold on tightly as the boat ping-ponged on the dark waters.

It wasn't long before she reached where the boat should've been. There was no sign of people in need. She halted the boat and rolled on the waves. Not too far ahead was the ferry—seemingly booting it now—and beyond that were a handful of smaller boats still visible. Everything was grey, the rain bouncing off the ocean, giving the effect of raining from above and below.

"Where did you go? Did you even see it?" Mandy asked herself.

Suddenly she felt a little silly. Must've been a trick of the eyes. Probably the fishing vessel had gotten in front of the ferry…though it sure as hell didn't look like that. What it looked like was the boat blinking out, like it went through an interdimensional gateway. She shook away the thought. Not so long ago she'd watched a YouTube video on why flights were always routed around a spot in the mountains called Paradigm Peak because passengers disappeared or winked out before coming back dead mid-flight. On the video, a once famous TV psychic spoke of a hotel lost to time called Camp Summit. It had spooked her out so much that she resorted to watching cat videos for the rest of the night.

But Paradigm Peak was about 500 miles away, so what happened here?

She sat there a moment feeling calm, despite the rocky waters and pounding rains. At least out here a giant moose or cougar couldn't get her. She watched the ferry until her gaze shifted to the shining black hump rising from the surf.

"Holy crow," she whispered, instantly recognizing what it was, though being mystified by its size.

8

One of the young moose climbed to its feet and strayed from its sibling and parent to consider a tipped over camping cooler a few yards from where they'd hunkered down. From the tree line above the moose, wolves, massive and skinny as malnourished cattle, watched for an opening. Not all animals had taken the change well and the wolves were the worst of the survivors—many species simply didn't survive, their bodies reacting as if poisoned rather than bolstered. They were muddy of mind and singularly focused on what might've once been a meal they'd steer clear of.

They charged, the only noises being the snapping of tree limbs and the grinding over gravel underfoot. The first wolf launched itself at the lowered neck of the youngling moose. It honked a great cry as teeth sunk. The second wolf aimed for the rump, tearing into the tough hide, reefing back and forth like it was a dog toy.

Barreling from the road, through trees, came the other two moose. The adult lowered its head and slammed its great rack into the wolf that had attached itself to the throat of its victim. One of the rack points found the wolf's left eye, pounding it back into the socket with enough force to pop it like an overripe blackberry. The wolf let go, and the moose began to stomp.

The bitten moose toppled to its side, while the

other young moose danced in panicked excitement. The big moose quickly shifted focus and charged at the animal still attempting to feast, even given the now impossible odds. The antlers lowered like a thorny snowplow blade. When they struck the wolf's side, the wolf's ribs rattled a bone song of pain before snapping out of tune. The wolf yipped and rolled. The adult moose stamped forward, roaring out a great honk that echoed as loudly as the air siren had.

In seconds, the fight was over. The wolves were dead. The young moose lay on its side, panting. The other two moose settled in next to it, indifferent now to the pounding rain and screaming wind. For the following hour, they sat as if awaiting the moment when their brethren's heart ceased beating, and its barrel chest refused to fill with air.

9

"How did we ever get talking about Kevin Bacon?" Lin said, a little louder than a whisper.

Lin had posted up beneath a cracked window, sitting on the stainless-steel dishwashing counter like she was lazily guarding the house, a cigarette steadily burning, one after another, and a can of beer in hand. George had fallen asleep immediately after eating a few handfuls of food, almost inhaling the stuff. Jacy was stretched out on the prep counter. Beyond the door, now and then, came the sounds of buzzing insects and indecipherable animal cries.

Without shifting her gaze from the yellowed wood of the ceiling fifteen feet above, Jacy said, "First I said my dad ate horse once. Then you said you ate crickets. Then I asked if you went to Africa before because I saw on YouTube this guy eating crickets, saying it was a delicacy, and that if Africans ate crickets more, they wouldn't starve so much—he was a dickhead. Then you said no. Then I asked where you ate the crickets. Then you said at a pop-up restaurant that showed up in Vancouver for a month one summer, for a story. Then I asked if you ever covered bigfoot. Then you said no, but you did a story on Ogopogo, which you said is kind of like BC's Loch Ness Monster. I asked if it was like a dragon. You said it was like a snake, then you said something about a lake. I don't remember what.

Then I said was it like the Graboids from *Tremors.* Then you said no; is that the one with Kevin Bacon. Then I said yes and that in *Friday the Thirteenth,* in Kevin Bacon's death scene the blood pump failed and the makeup guy had to blow through the tube from beneath the bed—my dad told me that. Then you said you had a boyfriend in college who looked like Kevin Bacon, but mostly in the nose."

"You have a good memory," Lin said, tossing her butt into the huge sink. She'd plugged it and ran about a quarter inch of water into the bottom.

"My dad says if I'd shut up more, I could have more things to hear and I'd be smart as Einstein in no time," Jacy said.

"You say your dad's on a cruise?" Lin said.

Jacy sighed. "Yeah, someone got sick and then the whole boat got sick. It's to make sure it doesn't catch everywhere and start something, like bird flu. That's what my mom said. My dad's sick, but not dying, just bad flu sick. That's what my mom said. I was real mad when they went without me, but now I'm glad it was an adult cruise."

"Interesting. I haven't heard anything about it on the news," Lin said. She sipped her beer, eyeing the wall clock.

"I tried to make them take me because I thought they were lying about there being no kids, but when I went on Reddit, there were people saying that Starry Eyes Cruises are like swingers' conventions."

Lin had to gulp down hard to avoid not spitting out the beer in her mouth.

"If they're doing that stuff, I don't want to know

nothing," Jacy said. "I closed out of Reddit and didn't look anymore."

"Gabriola Island is supposed to be a swingers' island," Lin said. "I don't know for sure, seems unlikely that a whole island that's barely an island—"

George cleared his throat, cutting off Lin. "Hey, there's something scratching," he whispered before nodding his chin to the door.

The barrier remained firm, but something was indeed scratching. It sounded much like a frantic cat, but one played in fast forward. The scratches sounded deeper, too, as if whatever was out there was really making a dent with every strike.

The trio silently watched the door rock with minute jerks. Sawdust began to puff out from beneath the door at the corners. Chunks of wood disappeared, and a pointy black snout pushed through. The fur was greasy. The animal voices were now undeniable. That was a huge rat, and that huge rat was not alone.

Lin popped from the counter, wide-eyed, scanning the large kitchen. "Jacy, cleaning supplies?"

Jacy, equally wide-eyed, pointed to the rack next to the linen closet at the far end of the kitchen. The rats had her momentarily speechless.

Lin broke through the kitchen. She reached the rack. The bleach would help. The jug of rubbing alcohol couldn't hurt. Leaned against the wall was a wide dry mop. An idea formed. She grabbed the bleach and rolled the ovular jug back across the room.

"Grab that!" she said.

Lin then took up the jug of rubbing alcohol and soaked the head of the dry mop. She set the jug aside and reached into her pocket for the lighter she'd stolen—unfortunately not a torch—when she'd grabbed the drinks and a pack of smokes.

George was on his feet. He'd picked up the bleach and was staring at the door. Jacy was next to him, popping around aimlessly, almost acting out her name.

"Jacy, grab that rubbing alcohol. Any glass bottles or jars in here?" Lin said as she crossed the room with the dripping mop.

"No," Jacy said. "I don't know." She hurried over the drip path left by Lin's mop and headed for the rubbing alcohol jug.

Lin bent before the door. A rat had chewed far enough to get its softball-sized head through. Hideous. She bent and flicked the lighter. She had to jerk away from the billowing flame the moment it lit. A second later she was standing straight and stabbing the broom against the door. The rat squealed for mercy as it burned. The scent was awful—equal parts pork drippings, burned hair, and sunbaked kitchen garbage.

She backed off then, fully aware a wooden door didn't appreciate fire. "George, check out that door," Lin said, nodding over her shoulder to the heavy steel door that led outside. She then looked at Jacy. "Splash some more on the mop head. Don't long pour it, kind of slosh it out."

"My neighbor one time lit a bonfire with gas and it trailed into the spout, then he got scared," Jacy sloshed cupfuls out of the large jug as she spoke, "and kicked the can, and fire shot out. All over the lawn, then a tree, then the fire department came, and they fined him like a thousand bucks."

The squeaky chatter of the rats resumed at full volume and Lin stabbed at the door that led into the dining room. Jacy quit sloshing out alcohol.

George figured out the pins to the lock and opened the outer door a crack, hand ready with the uncapped bleach jug. He scanned the area and his eyes stopped at the grease dumpster. Standing about six feet at its shoulders, a coyote had its head inside the huge steel bin. It jerked free when it finally sensed George, icky and sticky with golden brown ooze.

"Okay, no," George said.

Beyond the tarmac at the back of the hotel was a sea of mutilated rabbits, all of them huge, but no less dead for their size. Three more coyotes were chewing on the stringy red meat hiding behind the now pink fuzz. George closed the door and reinserted the pin.

"Well?" Lin said.

George shook his head. "Big coyotes."

"How big?" Jacy said.

"Big, big," George said.

"Space big?" Jacy said.

George nodded.

Lin began looking around the kitchen more. There were knives, but a lot of good that would do them. Not now anyway, though perhaps later.

"Jacy, man the mop," Lin said.

Jacy got bug eyes, splashed the mop head afresh,

and took the handle, immediately jamming it against the door. Lin hurried over to the linens and grabbed three white tea towels. Knives hung from a magnetic strip on the wall, and she took the three longest. She wrapped them and set them on a counter. She resumed her scan of the options. There was a tall stepladder stashed in a corner—given Mandy's height, there might be stepladders stashed all over the hotel. She looked to the grimy steel vent network overhead. It was old, the heavy looking stuff. The strapping was industrial thick and more hopeful for it. They'd never escape through household style vents, but this stuff…this stuff had promise. The venting disappeared through the wall into the dining room—hopefully above the dining room and beyond, to somewhere convenient and safe.

10

The moose had unintentionally visited the former library where the town's paperwork had been stored. The building had a cinderblock foundation with one of only a handful of proper basements in the entire town. The street it was on was about fifteen feet above sea-level, one of the highest points on the island—outside the big hill leading to the hot springs and the small mountains way out in the national park lands. The wooden siding of the building was in splintered tatters. Those cinderblocks were as much crumbled as whole. The doorway was caved in, the wrought iron handrail twisting like a gate across the passage.

"Get behind the wheel and be ready to take us away," Scotty said before hopping out of the heavy dodge.

"Me?" Miriam said.

Dillon was already out, his door left open as Scotty's had been. Miriam climbed down and then up into the driver's seat. She pulled her door closed and watched the men. They were efficient without looking rushed, lifting and tossing, lifting and tossing. Miriam turned her attention to the world around them—she was the getaway driver after all, and she might want to keep an eye on anything they might potentially need to flee from.

Several blocks behind the Dodge, a large figure burst from beside a house and began crossing the street in a sprint. Beyond sight at that distance, something like a rope lashed out—though it was impossible to wholly define—and the figure slammed hard, face down, before being reeled backward. The fall must have done some damage as there was no fighting the hold. The figure disappeared and left Miriam with only her imagination remaining to put together the pieces.

Someone had mentioned a spider when she'd been a part of a much larger group. Was Picture Island growing spiders *that* big? It was a tough idea to swallow, but with everything else going on it didn't exactly sound out of place.

She shook her head gently. If it weren't for the potential of this commission, she'd probably be going crazy. The impending paycheck was so, so big that it blinded all else. Hell, if it weren't for the commissions, she would've been safe and sound the first ferry off the island. Would she ever even have come back if it weren't for the potentially big ticket?

Yes.

She'd been curious and looking for an excuse.

"Curiosity killed the cat," she whispered. "But revenue brought it back."

The men had moved enough debris to get inside, but were still well within view, clearing a path. Hopefully everything would be plainly marked. She could almost see the wildly heavy, old-timey filing cabinets. There'd be a slip of paper in a cue card slot on the front of each drawer, marker faded but legible. The cards might say things like property taxes or deeds or who knew what. As long as it was obvious and the files were where they should be, this would be an easy-peasy trip.

She glanced out her window, out into the water a ways below. Distantly, she saw the shadow of the ferry. She then saw a great spout of water shoot up. In her life, she'd seen hundreds of whale spouts, none were even a tenth as large as this one. She swallowed. Were there beasts in the water too? Had whales become monstrous—more so than they already were?

How big did a whale have to get to sink a ferry?

"Not so big…not like it's a battleship."

Miriam kept her eyes pinned on the ocean until a loud, metallic clunking stole her attention. The mercenaries were stepping through the door with a large filing cabinet. The way the veins in their arms bulged told the tale of weight. Scotty set his end down and opened the back before picking his end up anew. Once they had an end inside, Dillon forced it the rest of the way, grunting gently beneath his breath. Without word to Miriam, the mercenaries returned to the former library. Within a minute, they were on their way out with another filing cabinet, this one chocolate brown rather than off-white. The cabinet was loaded. Again, they disappeared.

"No way we need all that," Miriam said, looking at the cabinets.

Scotty reappeared first with a large former banana box, still waxy even years after its initial use. Dillon came then and had a cracked blue laundry hamper loaded with paper.

Immediately after they got in, Miriam said, "I

saw a whale spout like you wouldn't believe."

Scotty was sitting shotgun. "To the hall and bunker, ma'am."

"No, the hotel first," Miriam said, pulling out onto the street, signal clicking with habit.

"That's not necessary," Dillon said.

"We promised Mandy. If she finds out we didn't go, do you think she'd make it easy to buy the hotel?" Miriam said, rolling toward the Picture House Lodge.

"She won't matter. There's a reason everything's coming by air," Dillon said.

Miriam squinted, looking into the rearview mirror, and then she got it. "Did you know about the whale? Are there more things that changed in the ocean?"

Dillon challenged her gaze.

"Jesus…you let all of them go out, and you knew?"

"Not our objective to assist those on the island." Scotty remained looking out his window as he spoke.

Miriam pulled a hard left toward the hotel. "Let me guess, easier for Cohagen to buy from relatives than from owners who might have attachments."

"That's beyond the scope of our mission," Dillon said.

Miriam reached the parking lot of the hotel and Scotty finally looked at her. "Ma'am, we have no business here."

"Good thing you put me at the wheel then," Miriam said and then stuck out her tongue.

Scotty snapped out a dirty hand and pinched her

tongue, even tugged it a little, before letting go. "Watch your mouth, civilian."

11

Denver took hold of the phone just as the ferry began to tip. He clutched tightly at the chunky plastic device, his hand paling at the effort. The steel of the vessel groaned, and the crowded passengers screamed and shouted. Dr. Goldstein had stumbled into the feet of the panicked throngs after the backs of his knees met the bumper of a Subaru and he flipped over the hood. The ferry rocked back and the SUV where Denver sat thumped hard enough to lift the driver's side wheels off the floor a few inches.

A steady moan played up Denver's throat. He clutched the phone tight to his chest. The ferry continued to rock but was slowly coming to rest evenly on the busy ocean. The engines flared again—obviously the captain had stalled things for a moment while the ship dipped and swayed, attempting to regain equilibrium.

Thud!

The impact was tremendous. The steel hull crunched, and vehicles skidded about the slick floor. The ramps to the upper level dropped, slamming into vehicles below. A woman took one of the ramps to the top of her head and the snap of her back was like kindling over a knee. The chaos redoubled and the captain got on the PA system, demanding that everyone go to the main deck for life vests and life rafts. One of the employees in an orange vest had a white life jacket in her hand as she ran by the back of the SUV. Denver swallowed in terror as his eyes met hers.

He'd never make it to a life raft.

He'd never get a life jacket—

The woman peeled back around the rear of the SUV and tossed the life jacket at him. "I'm sorry, I can't do more."

Denver put the phone in his pants pocket and quickly strapped into the vest. In those hectic moments, he didn't feel the pain of his missing foot. Those moments of terror took his mind away better than even the good dope he'd taken to deal with the lost appendage.

Another thump plowed into the ferry, sending it rocking sideways while completely halting the forward motion. Denver popped out of the back of the SUV as if sprung from an evacuation seat. He landed on the hood of the Subaru Dr. Goldstein had slipped over, smashing the windshield with his ass. From this vantage, he saw why the doctor hadn't returned to his vehicle. He was on the floor in a great puddle of dark, dark blood that stood out starkly against the pale blue paint.

Thud—crash!

Water poured over the stern and the ferry began to tip. Denver couldn't move. It was as if he'd been glued to the windshield. He looked around, panicked. There was nobody in any of the vehicles…almost nobody. A woman and three boys sat stoically in a car four rows down. A wooden cross hung from her rearview mirror. Denver wanted to scream at them, but was watching for death to come better or worse than rushing to meet it? Anything that could take down a ferry was apt to do quick work of lifeboats.

At this thought, Denver relaxed. He recalled his mother and was about to pull out the phone when the angle at which the ferry had tipped became extreme and vehicles began popping out. Denver slid in reverse, his eyes on the mother and her kids. A shaggy blonde boy of no more than five waved to Denver from the back seat. Denver lifted his hand in response.

His organs seemed to jump as the vehicle rocketed out in screeching reverse. The cool ocean jumped at him, instantly freeing him from the windshield. A dozen lifeboats floated not one hundred feet away. They were making distance and Denver watched them go, trying to ignore the fresh pain of the saltwater against the wound at the end of his leg.

The incredible orca surfaced, its massive jaws spread. Denver gasped, equal parts surprise, terror, and appreciation—the world wasn't ending for him without showing him something rarer than rare and all the more fantastic for it. It took four of the boats in a single gulp before dropping below. Within seconds, a geyser of water sent one of the life rafts high, high into the rainy grey sky. The thirty or so onboard swung arms and legs, pinwheeling crazily before dropping with great splashes.

Further ahead, a fishing vessel had turned back, assumedly to latch onto lifeboats and tug them along to the mainland. The orca seemed to understand this. They were smart to begin with, so what happened when the brain got super-sized?

"You don't need all that salt!"

Denver heard his mother's voice clear as day. It's what she always said to his father whenever he ordered fries in a meal, and always asked for extra salt. He'd grin and pour the extra salt over the already salty fries, winking at Denver's mother with the manner of taunt only a loving husband could get away with.

Denver reached into his pocket and hit the power button on the soaked phone. Distantly, the orca had resurfaced and was in the process of swallowing the fishing vessel that had been attempting heroism, as well as two more of the lifeboats and some of the people who'd come to be floating around like he was.

The waterproofing on the phone was fantastic and the satellite had him playing with full bars. He dialed the number he'd given out to all his buddies as a kid, the same number he'd called when he needed a ride home from baseball practice, the same number he'd called that time he and two other boys played a prank and were sent home from school. It rang and rang and rang and—

"Hello?" The voice was old and crackly but was the only thing Denver really needed in that moment.

"Hey, Mom, it's me."

"Oh, hey, can I call you back? I'm—"

"Not really. I'm going to die soon," Denver said, only truly acknowledging the fact the moment it came out of his mouth.

"What?"

"All that stuff about the space gator? Well, it's

all out of control. I'm floating in the Pacific and I'm already short a foot."

"Who do I call?" She was shrill, the words tumbling out of her.

"Nobody. There's nobody that can save me now."

The orca resurfaced, much closer than it had been, and swallowed ten boats in a single gulp. Suddenly, it seemed as if he was alone on the water. Though he heard a buzzing coming nearer.

"I'll call the coast guard! I'll—"

"I love you, Mom. Thought I better say that; one last time."

The way she spoke, it was clear she was shaking her head, her voice coming in waves. "No! No! I'll call! I'll get you help!"

"Won't help…I love you," Denver said, the words jammed in his throat. The whale was trolling, eyes above the surf, not thirty feet away.

"I love you too."

A shot rang out and, startled, Denver dropped the phone into the depths of the dark ocean beneath him. The whale jerked and a great wave buried him momentarily. Water filled his ears and mouth. He kicked—the pain was tremendous, but he reached the surf. The saltwater left his throat and chest in a gagging, wracking series of coughs. He blinked out at the rainy, barren world of the Pacific and wondered just what in the hell had saved him, at least momentarily.

12

Mandy had to kill the throttle only moments after getting moving again. She'd watched in stunned, cautious silence as the ferry rocked back and forth and the massive orca—had to be more than fifty feet long, perhaps sixty or sixty-five—dipped and rose, dipped and rose. The lifeboats had dropped like baby spiders from a hatched sac, fanning out over the rocky Pacific. It wasn't long after that that the ferry sank, sending vehicles out the back end like chunky diarrhea.

Things began to float and at first Mandy thought they were people. She throttled up and buzzed closer, though she was still more than one hundred yards out from the action. That's when she saw the orca rise with its great jaws split wide, swallowing away at least two lifeboats. The following splash was big enough that it sent the speedboat—even at a goodly distance—into convulsions. She had to throttle down again, barely clinging to the steering wheel and the half-cab's frame. Her legs were spread, and her knees were bent. So she didn't lose it in the upheaval, the rifle was pinched against a steel wall with her right foot.

Mandy waited for the boat to settle and decided, before continuing, she'd better check beneath the trapdoors of the deck for damage or flooding. The door sitting at about the mid-way point was almost certainly the engine compartment. She grabbed onto a galvanized steel ring and yanked. The hot oil smell blasted at her on a heatwave. No steam or smoke, however.

"Good," she said and then had a thought.

If the boat did go down, she didn't want to go with it. She dropped the door and crouched to get below the dashboard. Here was another hatch. This door was lighter and came open with clamps rather than a ring. Within, she found two cob-webby life vests, both red and blue, both too big for her. She took the smaller of the two and clipped into it. If she'd had an identical twin, the twin could've fit in with her, no problem.

At the controls again, the engine growling gently, she reassessed the situation. It appeared only a few lifeboats remained afloat.

"Jeepers," she whispered.

Selflessly, she pounded the throttle and cut over the rocky waves. Within seconds, the orca was rising again, pointing at something floating.

"Denver?"

The splash nailed her and she ducked beneath the wash, throttling down again. The water in the boat was up to her knees and the engine had begun hiccupping. The orca resurfaced and was gliding toward Denver. Without thinking, Mandy scooped up her rifle and began mentally timing the waves. Probably whales were about as tough as tractor tire rubber. That left one option currently available to her. A single glassy target.

On a downstroke of the ocean, she exhaled and fired at the whale's huge eye. A half-second later, the beast jerked and splashed, sending out a fresh wave. Denver disappeared and the boat's engine quit on her. The water was up to her thighs.

"Denver?" she shouted.

He popped up. She looked to the rowboats. They were full of water, but not sinking—unlike the speedboat, which was now floating on borrowed time. The orca came up from directly under Denver. Mandy took her second shot. The angle wasn't great. She didn't get to aim. The rifle was sopping. The ocean was rocking. That shot barked and then buzzed, moving on a line so damned perfect it was as if she'd wished it there rather than shot it. The orca's left eye burst inward a moment before the beast splashed heavily back into the ocean. Its cry was huge and horrible. The wave back-washing over her was even bigger. The speedboat disappeared beneath her, dragging down the rowboats. Her fingers lost grip on the rifle.

She had no time to gather an extra chest-full of air and went under on the verge of panicking. The pressure in her ears was great. Somehow, she'd gone way, way down, perhaps fifteen feet. Mandy's chest banged with ache as she surged toward the grey light above. It might be futile to extend life this little bit, but her survival instincts gave her no choice. It wasn't ready to die yet. She wasn't ready to die yet.

13

Chuck went upstairs every ten minutes to look out the windows of the old hall above the bunker. Someone, he wasn't sure who, had been keeping up the bunker irregularly. The cans had semi-recent labels, and the old TV had a bulky DVD/VCR combo hooked up. He'd had the radio on low the entire time, listening for news about what was happening on Picture Island for more than an hour when there was finally an emergency update.

"After only just recently surviving the unthinkable, locals on Picture Island have been quarantined today. It appears there's been an anthrax attack. We don't know who or why, but we do know passage to and from the island is prohibited. And on top of that, given the violent weather, all their methods of communication are down. Though I'm guessing there's always the shortwave option," the nasally sounding man said through the tinny little speaker on the paint-spattered portable radio—the ghost of an RCA label rode front and center, obviously someone had knocked off the lettering. "According to sources, everything is under control, though no timeline…"

This was so incorrect that it had to be purposeful. And, although he'd thought it impossible, something was jamming the shortwave signal. He'd blown off the dusty old Grundig on the bunker desk and had spun the sum of the entire airwave spectrum only to find nothing was coming in. A conspiracy was brewing, though he perhaps understood why. Outside those living on Picture Island, the only thing knowing about these beasts would do was get folks worried.

Chuck was upstairs now, having given up on both radios and the TV. He was looking out the window of the door when another thought struck him hard enough to liquify his guts. "Other people knowing would keep the government from nuking Ghost Clearing," he said, thinking aloud.

Jesus. Did that kind of thing happen in real life?

Thankfully the train of thought was interrupted when he saw Theo Rissmiller and his kids breaking from a backyard. Theo had a weed sprayer and his eldest daughter held a tall butane torch.

"Just what the—?" Chuck began but was silenced when a frog lashed out a tongue at them.

Father and daughters got busy quick. The sprayer doused the thing and the eldest lit the torch, touching it to the flow. That wasn't Round-Up in that sprayer. The frog lit and went hopping off, aflame and squealing.

"Now that's some family teamwork," Chuck said and opened the door, rifle in his grip. "Bring it in!" he called out to the foursome.

The two youngest sprinted straight across the parking lot. Father and his eldest moved quickly, though much more cautiously. The youngest reached the door, stinking of piss and gasoline.

"Straight through to the basement. No stopping," Chuck said, pointing.

Within seconds, Theo and his eldest arrived and

Chuck closed the doors behind them.

"Looks like you've seen some things," he said.

Theo Rissmiller said, simply, "Boy," elongating the vowel sound.

14

The giant, still-growing orca blinked rapidly, trying to force the pain and cloudiness from its eyes. It wasn't working. It turned away from the fight to regain its composure, heading straight east. It had to rely solely on its ears, and distantly, it heard things amid the quiet mass of water. In something like a panic, though not quite, as it had a great deal of hereditary skills to fall back upon, the giant beast—now almost sixty feet long—trailed after the sounds as if they might answer why its eyes had gone black.

Being a juvenile, basically a newborn, the orca hadn't had time to come to a full understanding, to be one with the scenery, to swim with it rather than against it. A new need overshadowed the fear and the orca rose. Time was passing quickly, and it had gone close to one hundred miles since being shot that second time. It cleared its blowhole in a fantastic wave before taking deep, deep breaths above the rocky surf.

Within thirty seconds, the beast was back underwater. The whale song it had heard had ceased. Crazed with uncertainty, the orca swam hard, cutting the Pacific as if it held zero resistance. Nine minutes later, it resurfaced for air before screaming back down to the depths, pushing deeper this time, deeper than it had ever been.

Veering south, the orca powered on. The hours

mounted. Regular visits to the surface garnered no attention. Its energy began to deplete by the third day. On the tenth day of steady, panicked travel, the orca began to slow down. It had grown to full-size. It was as long as the longest blue whale ever recorded but nearly twice as heavy. It opened its mouth regularly, chancing at sustenance; it had never learned to catch using only sound. The constant pain and terror had come to depress the great monster, ravaging it from the brain out.

By the sixteenth day, the beast rose for breath and instantly heard another boom—the same kind that had stolen its eyesight. A fresh wave of panic took over and the orca dove. It went deeper and deeper. Its ears ceased function. Its lungs burned for air. And still, it dove from the painful memory and the chances of still yet more to come: more agony, more uncertainty, more terror, more loneliness.

At 2,500 feet beneath the surface, the orca's struggling lungs collapsed. Other organs began bleeding as if squeezed like a sponge. Long after things would settle on Picture Island, the giant orca was dead and drifting like a buffet table for many, many hours. Tides played the corpse until the coldest of cold seemed to drag it in for an embrace. The orca rolled along the ocean floor for six minutes before finding another precipice and dropping, dropping, dropping, the latest meal offering to creatures of the Mariana Trench.

Within seconds, many of those creatures set to feasting upon the otherworldly flesh.

15

Lin quit lifting as George pushed the bleach bottle ahead of him into the dusty, greasy airduct. The duct was wider than it was high, which would allow George and Jacy to shimmy smoothly, but would surely cause Lin a little trouble. This was the kind of situation not discussed at the gym— swimsuit season, wedding season, finally divorced season, sure, but there was no escaping through a ceiling duct season.

"At least it's not as dark as the beetle tunnels," George said; there was something like terror hiding beneath his words.

Lin heard it and had to shake it away as she lifted Jacy into the shadowy vent. Jacy had the knives wrapped in the tea towels in a tight, one-handed grip, on account of that Lin would have to use all her upper body strength and then some to pull herself into the vent. Thankfully, the baby weight had mostly fled—aside from her chest, which had begun to leak some after hearing the rats squeak beyond the door. The sound had triggered memories of Baby June whining for a breast. If Jacy or George noticed any dampness, they were polite enough to keep it to themselves.

"Make some space between. We don't want too much weight on each section," Lin said, eyeing the door.

They'd left the flaming mop in a puddle of

alcohol, but the door was in rough shape. One part burned and one part chewed. Here and there, little faces were poking through. Noises had also begun to come from the heavy steel door that led outside. Thumping and scratching, nothing any of them were about to investigate.

"Is three good?" Jacy said over her shoulder.

She was beyond Lin's view currently, but Lin guessed Jacy meant three pieces of duct and said, "Yeah, should be."

Lin exhaled a breath before placing the stepstool on top of the chair, which was on top of a counter. The chair was sturdy, but only three or four feet had room to fit on the seat of the chair. She closed her eyes. No matter what she had to deal with from here on, it couldn't be worse than the spider.

The door creaked before cracking. A foot-squared chunk fell into the kitchen and a parade of enormous rats scurried through like floodwater through a busted levy.

"Fuck. Fuck."

Lin climbed up and the stepstool instantly began swaying.

"Fuck."

She gave a single glance back to the rats before hopping. Her feet sent the stool flying and the chair tumbled. She was in the vent up to her bellybutton, her legs swinging beneath, pedaling for purchase.

"You okay?" Jacy said.

Lin couldn't answer. She grunted and clenched. Her vision glazed and she thought of her family, she could see them, a million miles from this goddamned hellhole of an island. Not getting back was not an option. Not getting up into the crummy vent was not an option. No great adrenaline rush came to assist her, and she had to rely on whatever energy remained in the tank.

She slipped, the vent catching at her armpits. Her breaths came out in tiny, haggard sips. She glanced down and the rats had spotted her. They raced to the counter where the chair had been. The lead beast leapt, a minor scratch raking across the bottom of her foot, and she jerked her legs away, inadvertently lessening her precarious hold.

They were on her then; their claws digging, their noses sniffing, and their teeth dragging. Lin screamed.

Hands clutched her armpits, digging painfully into the currently taught wells of flesh. Jacy began reefing. George was at least fifteen feet away, pulling on an old phoneline.

"Oww!" Jacy whined but did not let go.

One of the rats on Lin's legs bit into her ankle before her heel made contact with a beady eye. The rat screeched, flying across the kitchen. She was up again, now past her bellybutton. Her hands slapped at the walls of the vent for grip while her legs continued swimming out behind her, anything that had clung until then had fallen away.

"Go! Go!" she said the moment she was all the way in.

Jacy balled up and rolled to face away. She grabbed the two running strands of phoneline and said, "Pull me!"

At the other end of the vent, George got busy, as if bringing in a fish with a broken reel. Lin squirmed after her, glancing back every few seconds to be sure the rats didn't get in. At about the midway point, she reached the knives Jacy had left behind—probably to rescue her. She stuffed two down the back of her pants and the third she put down her shirt. All remained wrapped in tea towels.

Before she got moving, she cast another glance back. A rat was trying to do a chin-up into the vent, not so differently than she had been. She faced forward, and the kids were gone, which was good. It meant there was a way out at the end of the vent, though perhaps it was only a bend. She began squirming again, writhing with manic desperation, trying to score any iota of speed available.

A sense of relief bloomed when George reappeared, upside down. He hung from the ceiling of the vent and simply watched. Lin wasted no breaths and charged as fast as was possible. The grime of the dusty grease clung to her, streaking the pale flesh of her arms and face. Her clothing had grown stiff with the myriad events of the last twenty or so hours. The stink emanating from her armpits would've been embarrassing in *any* other situation.

George popped away a couple moments before Jacy appeared. "There's rats behind you," she said.

As if Lin didn't know. As if she hadn't heard them, hadn't felt the gentle vibrations as their claws raked at the steel floor of the vent. Jacy disappeared as Lin reached the home stretch. The rat sounds were very, very close. She didn't dare look.

At least not until one grabbed onto the tread of her shoe. It threw off her rhythm just enough to slow her a hair. Maybe five more collective jerk-slap-shimmies and her head would touch the end. She felt a second rat, this one clung onto the ankle hem of her pants. The only saving grace—for the moment—was that she was moving too much for them to do any more than cling onto her.

Hands shot down from above just before she reached the end. She stopped and the rats instantly began to climb her legs. A third rat found her, this one scooting up her pants, but only getting as far as its face.

"Get off!" Lin shouted.

Jacy's hands lifted, and Lin slipped.

"Not you, the rats!" Lin said.

Jacy reached back down and pulled. She grunted and whined steadily. Lin's body had to go all but limp below the waist while her tired arms pulled, fingers pinched into seams in the vent for purchase. Lin looked at the darkening sky above the hotel. A new trouble would be hitting soon—assuming they got out of danger from within the hotel. Night was coming. On an average day, screwing around outside after dark in a remote, semi-northern Canadian town was an unwise idea as it was.

Jacy roared, lifting with all she had until Lin's knees finally got under her. She popped upright. There was George, ready with the bleach jug. Once Lin was standing straight, though still in the vent, George began splashing the rats. One had gotten as high as her lower back, and at first it appeared the bleach was going to do nothing, but after two long, long seconds, the rat screeched and fell away like salted leeches peeling from a swimmer's flesh. George poured more on the other two as Lin got her body up and bent at the waist to fall over the vent's opening—thankfully, the hooded cover had only clung by a single rusty screw before George had reached it.

Lin flopped onto the stony rooftop and rolled, kicking her legs. Unaware the rats had already fallen away.

"I'm almost out of bleach!" George said.

"We need to block the hole!" Jacy said.

Lin registered the reality of the moment and looked around the flat roof. Not far away was an old tire rim with a steel post welded to it. On top of the post was a battered old TV antenna. That would perhaps do. She rolled to her feet and found her steps shaky and weak. Her hands were steady, though her arms were like rubber. She latched on and tried to lift the post on the rim and found it heavier than expected.

George tossed the jug down into the vent and stumbled in reverse. Jacy grabbed him and they watched in wide-eyed terror, unaware of Lin for the moment. Three rats poked their ugly, greasy heads topside. One of them had fur that had been bleached to a pinkish hue around its eyes.

"Help!" Lin said.

George broke from Jacy's embrace and tried to pick up the heavy tire rim. He grunted, discovering the unexpected weight while momentarily stalling Lin's forward motion.

"That won't block it!" Jacy said, running to help.

"We aren't blocking it," Lin said through clenched teeth.

Jacy and George had the end up and the trio ran

to the vent. One of the rats climbed over, and then a second, a third, a fourth.

"Lift high and let it go once I get it straight over," Lin said.

On target, as a writhing mass of rats scrambled at the steel walls of the vent, they dropped the ancient antenna stand and the vent separated, dropping down into the restaurant's dining area. One rat remained clinging. Lin, channeling her frustrations, wound back and punched the rat in its wet nose. It lost hold and fell into the hotel.

With the vent gone, the smoke from the burning dining room was free to rise.

"Shit," Lin said.

"Help!"

Jacy was on her back; one of the rats had come for her while the other two had disappeared. The rat was swiping at her, its claws had already raked three ugly divots in her cheek by her ear. Froth oozed from the corners of its mouth, and its eyes were cloudy with bleach burns. George grabbed at the rat, choking it as he reeled it away. A huge thing, like a Maine Coon cat, but nasty. He shook and shook. Jacy below, staring up. Motion claimed Lin's attention. One of the rats broke over the side of the building.

"Die, rat!" George wailed before flinging the unmoving beast off the roof.

Lin looked down over the far side of the roof and saw the massive coyotes George had mentioned. They saw her as well. There was no way to go down the back.

"Did you see a way down?" Lin said, stumbling

in reverse to Jacy and George, who'd huddled up, holding each other where they sat in the rooftop gravel.

Smoke began to billow. Two windows shattered below. They couldn't stay up there long, soon Picture House Lodge would be no more. Barely over the crackling and chittering from within the building, an engine sounded. Lin jogged to the front edge of the hotel and began waving her arms.

"Hey! Hey!"

A Dodge SUV had only just pulled out of the parking lot and was rolling away. Within seconds, it was an entire block from them. From her vantage, Lin could see every turn it took. Hell, from up there, she could see pretty well the whole town. It looked empty, though here and there spider webs thick as clothesline caught the greyed light playing through the clouds.

"At least it quit raining," Jacy said.

Lin said nothing to this and stalked the rooftop looking for another way down. Getting ahead of herself, she wondered what came after that. Where could they go on an island infested with giant things? The easy answer was to hide in a house, any house...but what else might be hiding in a house?

She reached the southern edge of the roof and saw nothing useful. She scanned where she'd last seen the Dodge and discovered it parked at a building about a mile away. Give or take. She'd have to get them there, somehow, and preferably before full dark set in.

Lin hurried back to look out at the parking lot. There were a couple trucks out there, if one of them had keys in it…

"Jacy, where's that wire George used to pull you through the vent?" she said, an idea forming as she spoke. Maybe, just maybe, there was hope yet.

16

The digital clock on the dash of the Dodge flipped a number to 7:58 the moment Miriam put the shifter to park. The engine rumbled, and faintly, the CBC News was on the air from the stereo. Miriam attempted to ignore the big men staring daggers at her and increased the volume. The man speaking was talking about the clearing weather on the mainland and the variety of outlying islands—unmentioned, though included, was Picture Island.

"And now for the ongoing story. An anthrax outbreak on Picture Island has all ferry travel restricted, as well as consumer vessel visits. Residents currently on the mainland or on Vancouver Island are being told not to go home, even now as the water will calm into the night. So far, the information is minimal and our efforts to reach anyone with authority on the scene have been futile. Contact once again appears to have been knocked out from the island—you'll recall that recently they dealt with what appeared to be an alien lifeform, and speculation is that the current communications result from unacknowledged damage caused by the creature…"

Miriam fingered the button off. A cover-up was at hand, at least currently, and she guessed that made sense. Nobody not on the island needed to know, not yet. But what of the ferry load who should've arrived by now, or would soon?

"What exactly is in the water?" Miriam said.

"That has nothing to do with real estate," Scotty said.

The clock on the dash now read 8:03. A dining room window shattered, and smoke poured out of the hotel. Miriam clicked her tongue off the roof of her mouth.

"Guess they're not here," she said and pulled the shifter to drive and wound a large U-turn, taking them to about ten feet from the front entrance of the building.

The streets were empty. Those in the vehicle were silent aside from Scotty dictating a turn to Miriam. Dillon hadn't spoken since Miriam decided she'd go against the plan, taking them to Picture House Lodge in the first place. Once into the parking lot at the community hall and the bunker hidden beneath, Scotty reached over and killed the engine, withdrawing the keys from the ignition.

Through the doors of the hall, Chuck O'Shea was visible, leaning around the doorframe. He was armed and all the glass at the front of the hall was intact, which gave Miriam a much-needed shot of faith in the operation. Next to Dillon all this time, she'd never considered that something might get her, but seeing Picture House Lodge on fire, and registering how little the mercenaries cared about human life made her reconsider the situation. How tough was it to get another realtor to fill out paperwork?

Before they had a chance to get out of the Dodge, Dillon's tablet pinged. No video call, only a message.

"The choppers will depart at oh-seven hundred. Satellite imagery suggests the ranger station in the national park is gone," Dillon said.

"What would…was it the moose? Or are there huge bears?" Miriam said, terror on her words.

Dillon put the tablet away. "It appears the gigantism is not working well with bear species."

"I heard Mr. Cohagen already has a giant bear in the works," Scotty said before getting out.

"What the hell does that mean?" Miriam said.

Dillon did not answer her.

17

The silver, $190,000 Ricco car pulled into the Taco Bell drive thru. The car was white, with white-tinted windows. The entire body was a solar panel. The tech wasn't quite perfected, but the battery charged up to almost 50% on solar after about ten hours under the sun.

"I ordered online. For Richter Cohagen."

"Yes, yes, sir. It's ready. Pull on up," said the voice through the rusty menu box.

Richter Cohagen was known to the local Taco Bell, as well as the local Burger King, Starbucks, and Jack in the Box. The first few times he'd come—he wasn't local to Barstow, California—the employees thought his name was a prank when it popped up on the screen and ignored the orders. That was years ago, he was now accepted, though no less revered. He had enough money to end world hunger, clean everyone's drinking water, and install opportunities for minority groups to sit at the same tables as their white counterparts. He did none of this, of course. Instead, he used family money to have scientists make cars, plan out strange utopian societies, and research biological oddities. In his spare time, he went on podcasts to discuss nonsensical theories on why indigenous locals in the Third World had less, without acknowledging Western exploitation, and the positive effects of digging tunnels beneath cities to sell more real estate at affordable prices.

"I love this car," the young, pimply teen said from the window after handing out Cohagen's meal.

"Yes, of course," Cohagen said and pulled away.

As he drove, heading out of the city directly north, into blank yellow desert, he had his hand in the bag. He withdrew a taco that was only greasy meat and bread, and bit into one end. The trip to his research facility took about twenty-two minutes if he drove a hair beyond the speed limit. And, of course, he slowed down once departing the cracked asphalt of the two-lane highway to take a dirt road he'd had cut when he first brought in blindfolded Mexicans to build his facility.

At the end of the road—which looked like a long, rancher laneway—was a single off-white trailer. Cohagen hit the brakes and pressed the button affixed to the sun visor above his head. The trailer tilted smoothly upward, revealing the grated steel platform beneath. He drove onto the platform and parked. The hollowed trailer dropped over him and the vehicle. A high-powered vacuum sucked away all the dust particles before the platform began to lower. Seventy feet below the surface, Cohagen's car shuffled in next to nine other vehicles—lesser Ricco models—and a fleet of all-white helicopters. He stood from the car with his drink and the garbage from his meal.

The walls were cement, rising twenty-five feet to cement ceilings. Mounted at regular intervals were monitors outside doors. The monitors displayed what was happening within the rooms. Cohagen had a theory about windows and that the fewer windows a research facility had, the better. Just a *feeling* he had.

At the third door, Cohagen flashed his eyes over a sensor, and the door opened, a speaker playing the same whoosh-squeak noise from the original *Star Trek* series. The two women and one man in lab coats were already turned to face him.

"Everything is set for your flight to the BC facility," one of the women said.

"They've also informed us that everything is ready to transport to Picture Island," the man said.

"The weather is cooperating and will through the next three days," the other woman said.

It was important that they all add something to the message, as Cohagen was fickle and replaced employees without much consideration. He and the team of mercenaries under his employ were the only ones permitted to come and go from the facility. The scientists came to the facility blindfolded and were handcuffed by a litany of NDAs, though were sufficiently compensated for their efforts.

Cohagen nodded steadily as he listened. He'd opened the Canadian compound after the Canadian Military collected the corpse of what appeared to be a prehistoric she-bear. It took a little palm greasing, but Cohagen purchased the rights to the frozen beast and left it with the military up there until he could get his facility built just south of the Garibaldi Provincial Park and east of the Pitt River Hot Springs. There was not a residential building for about one hundred miles, and what was between the facility and civilian activity was a whole lot of trees and mountains on every side. Still, Cohagen being as paranoid as he was, he hid the facility. Rather than situating the access point beneath a trailer, he put it beneath a huge slab of plastic polymer painted to look like the rest of the valley. The moment before a Ricco chopper landed, the false earth rose a foot and slipped aside. The labs were only thirty feet below thanks to the extreme pain involved in digging into a mountainside. Unlike the California facility, which featured a host of projects, the British Columbia facility was dedicated to the study of giant beasts and petri dish reproductions of giant beasts.

And not only of the recently—comparatively—deceased she-bear; though attempts at creating new life from fossilized DNA had so far proven fruitless. Cohagen had never spoken it aloud—though all who knew of the studies suspected it—he was a big fan of the *Jurassic Park* movies and was dead certain he could've made the theme park turn huge profits—though some also whispered that they thought he would like to own dinosaurs, just so he could watch people succumb to their power.

"When do I head to Canada?" Cohagen said.

"Whenever you like," the first woman said.

"Better tonight," the man said.

"Than tomorrow," the second woman said.

18

Mandy floated for a time indiscernible to her before the realization struck that she might not die out there, that she might in fact get lucky enough to die on land, eaten by a jumbo cougar or coyote or who knew what. The lifejacket was up around her ears and had her leaning back in a way that dictated her stroke, or rather, lack thereof. She put her back to the east and kicked her feet. The sun was a sinking orange ball beyond the dissipating clouds. Every third wave washed over her but were mostly sending her where she wanted to go. Now and then she jerked around to see over a shoulder to correct her angle.

From the shore, a gathering of seals barked with great fervor and a few times they'd popped up next to her like inky jump scares and she'd gasp before breaking into laughter muddy with tears. She had to remind herself that it was almost certainly to the good that these animals—these regular-sized animals—were with her. If they were out, strolling, curious as stray cats, that probably meant there were no clearly visible predators. Had she done enough damage to the massive orca to send it away? She had no way of knowing beyond surviving one minute after another.

Mandy had to rest her legs. The rain had stopped, and the waves had lessened some. The sun had fallen further, was now a red, red fireball. All around her was tinted to a bloody hue, the shadows playing up the contrasts in a postcard palette. She floated, bobbing on the waves; gazing into this view had been one of the reasons she'd stayed on Picture Island all these years.

"Red sky at night, floater's delight," she said and took up kicking anew.

She was dog tired and imagined a helpful dolphin coming along to cart her on her merry way. She'd never actually seen the TV show *Flipper*, nor the movie, but understood enough to get that it was like *Lassie,* with a dolphin. Mandy closed her eyes and imagined grabbing the snout of a friendly creature as it cut through the waves and took her home. All the way home, right to the doorstep of the Picture House Lodge, where, somehow, her bed would be right there in the foyer awaiting her appearance.

"Home," she said, spitting saltwater as she did so.

Was there a home left?

She guessed not. Probably she'd be lucky to get anything from Richter Cohagen. And just what in the hell did he want with Picture Island? Some folks had too much money and collected oddities, that would be the best-case scenario. She doubted that likelihood. People like Richter Cohagen were insane, but their money kept everyone around them not only silent to the fact but encouraging of their asinine ideas. She hoped he bought the whole fucking island and then bought the farm while on it.

"Get eaten by a giant…whatever."

Mandy glanced over a shoulder to correct her

path—at least she could now make out shapes on the pier—and kicked harder. The sun wouldn't be up long and if she did make it to land, she wanted to see what she might want to watch out for, rather than walking right into the maw of some mega-sized monster.

19

The exhaustion hit George about a half-second after scaling down the side of the burning Picture House Lodge and sprinting to the carport of the nearest house. It appeared none of the animals in the vicinity had heard them flee—good thing because George was now bent over his knees gasping great gulps of air. He stared at his shoes. They were splotchy with browned blood over brown mud. Scuffs scarred the rubber around the sides and a tear had opened above the big toe of his left foot.

While stuck at the hospital, Carole had given him her wallet to buy some new things. He had taken Alexis on the Sky Train in Vancouver, riding much, much longer than necessary for the fun of it, and then to thwart the impending boredom that awaited them. They'd gone to the mall. At Footlocker, he and Alexis took advantage of the buy one get one deal on sneakers. Part of him had wanted to stick it to Carole. There were Air Jordans that were more than $300—he knew they went way higher if he could shop online—but $300 for shoes seemed just too outrageous. He was upset about Josie and his parents and then about Shane, losing all those people in a short time, and then being taken away from his girlfriend felt like a great big shit heap weighing down on him. Add that he had to hang around the boring hotel and the even more boring hospital, all the while playing babysitter to his little sister, George wanted to lash out. But none of it was Carole's fault, not really. He'd settled with orangey-white Puma sneakers. They featured ribbons of red suede and had looked like pale grapefruit rind beneath peach fuzz. Now, here they were, they'd been soaked, muddied, coated in bug guts, covered in dust, in grease, in blood, and all that together made them fit for the trash heap. It was enough that George wanted to cry out, perhaps break something.

He didn't and leaned against the vinyl siding of the bungalow beneath the carport. Jacy was at the door of the house, testing the lock. Lin was in the front seat of an older Honda Accord, obviously looking for keys. Where she expected to go, George had no clue. Probably it was the ability to move with an idea of protection. If the bigger of the animals they'd seen stepped on an Accord, they were as good as cooked anyway.

"Locked," Jacy said after coming to stand in front of George. "My dad says people in small towns always talk about not having to lock their doors, but everybody does it. He says if people have to pine for the good old days, they should go to the park and sit on a bench…because park benches are sometimes old and sometimes pine."

"What about under that?" George said.

There was a plastic rock sitting inconspicuously at the lip of the driveway in the yellowy-green grass.

Jacy wasted not a breath and hurried over to it. She picked it up and looked beneath. There was an indent in the lawn, but nothing more. She flipped over the rock and discovered a sliding compartment.

She slipped it open.

"Key!" she said and dropped the rock before hurrying to the door.

"Shh," Lin said before gently closing the Honda's driver's door.

Jacy put the key to the lock and turned the handle. It opened, letting out a heady waft of onion. Through the door to the left was a staircase that led downward to a four-foot crawlspace of grey cement. Straight on were three stairs with green indoor/outdoor rug. Jacy led, George followed, and Lin brought along the caboose. The steps upward took them into a kitchen decked out in 1970's chic: golden rod linoleum, a minty green fridge and oven, a Formica table with a loose steel band running the perimeter, and faded yellow cabinets. On the stove was a big pot. On the counter next to it was a ladle. Jacy opened the lid on the pot and the onion scent intensified.

"Soup," she said. "Mandy makes soup some days in these stupid bowls where the cheese sticks, and then when I have to wash them, the cheese floats in the water like dead stuff and makes me gag when I touch it."

"Won't have to worry about that now," Lin said absently.

Jacy made a face. George looked out the window. The hotel was ablaze, its flames licking high enough that they'd have been cooked already, had they stayed. On top of it all, nobody was coming to the rescue. No, Jacy wouldn't have to worry about Mandy's soup anymore.

"So, what do we do now?" Jacy said.

Lin stepped beyond the linoleum of the kitchen to the worn shag of the living room and a hallway to her left. The living room had two large couches, a recliner chair, and a massive Samsung flatscreen. When it came to updates, the homeowner had their priorities sorted. Lin flipped a light switch.

"I'm thinking we find a set of keys for the car and then hunker down close to a door," Lin said.

"At least the power's still on," George said. "The gator cut the power last time."

"I wouldn't rely on that. Who knows what will happen. Probably we ought to gather anything that might look useful." Lin pulled the wrapped knives out from the back of her pants. "These hardly feel like enough."

"They're real sharp though," Jacy said. "Mandy can…" she trailed.

George squinted then. "Think Mandy got on the ferry?"

"Seems like everyone did," Lin said.

Jacy pouted. "My aunt and uncle left me behind then. Nobody wants me anywhere."

George grabbed onto her and held her. She held him back. Lin stepped to the hallway and discovered three doors. One was a small bathroom with insulation-pink fixtures, another was a busy office with a spot where a laptop had been, and the third was the master bedroom. The shelves and dresser were littered with porcelain hedgehogs. On the nightstand next to a lamp was a book on how faith could cure anything, from AIDS to cancer to depression.

"Hope you never get sick," Lin whispered before

opening a dresser drawer.

"What?" Jacy said, now behind her.

"Nothing. Look in these drawers for the keys, or a gun," Lin said.

The longer they moved around the small house, the more comfortable they became. George was the first to take an extended seat. He stretched out on one of the living room couches while Lin and Jacy continued searching the house. The blinds were drawn over the bay window, but the yellowy light of the streetlamps shined through. He closed his eyes, but sleep did not come to him. The dark had him thinking, remembering the tunnels and those huge insects. The thoughts made him want to scream all over again. He did not. Instead, he listened; to his comrades and to the world beyond the walls, he listened.

"Nothing?" Lin said.

They'd found a couple hockey sticks and a dozen knives, if they wanted more of them, and ones significantly duller than those from Mandy's kitchen. There'd been no guns or rifles, not even a bow and arrow, not even a slingshot.

"No. Maybe they took everything like that for in case they ran into a monster on the way to the boat. My dad says you'd rather be caught with a gun than without one…but always in a nasal voice. He says stuff like that when he thinks it's stupid, but it wouldn't be stupid to have guns now," Jacy said.

"I guess…not sure how much good they'd do anyway," Lin said before stretching out on the second couch and taking up the TV remote. She turned on the TV only to discover there was nothing of local interest, only streaming options. "Shit. I feel really disconnected."

None of them still had their cellphones and the home's computer was gone. There was a clock radio in the bedroom, but nobody was talking about Picture Island with any certainty, and mostly the information was dead wrong.

"Me too," Jacy said, and surprisingly stopped there.

Lin opened the Netflix app. Two profiles appeared: Joan and 2. She selected Joan and the preview for *When Calls the Heart* began. Lin quickly lowered the volume and flipped down to the first row of options.

"I think we should stay in this room—outside bathroom breaks—and be quiet until daylight," Lin said.

On top of not bettering the weaponry situation, they also hadn't discovered any car keys. Going out at night seemed downright suicidal given the current state of Ghost Clearing.

Jacy flopped onto the recliner and put it back. "Fine by me," she said before stretching out a long yawn. "We going to watch something or you going to scroll all night? My mom always says that to my dad when he looks through every option and then gives her the remote when he can't decide what he wants."

Lin tossed the remote into Jacy's lap. "You pick. I need tea or coffee, something."

Jacy began flipping and stopped at *Derry Girls*. "My mom loves this show, even my dad likes it, but I don't really get it and sometimes I don't understand what the hell they're saying but it's still English."

Lin said nothing to that as she began searching the cupboards for teabags. The teapot was on the counter. She found a mixer box of Tetley and went with lavender. "You want tea?"

Jacy pulled a face, scrunching her expression toward her nose. "Uh uh," she said. "I don't like tea. The aftertaste is yucky."

"That's why you put something in it to sweeten it. George, are you awake?" Lin said. The electric kettle was on and quickly warming.

"Is there honey?" George said without opening his eyes.

"You're awake," Jacy said.

George squinted past his feet to Jacy on the recliner. "Yeah, but I'm beat."

Lin opened the pantry door. The closet was old, the shelves were solid wood with floral patterned wallpaper over them. On the second shelf from the floor was a 15KG bucket of Dutchman's Gold, raw honey.

"Found honey," Lin said.

She grabbed the handle and dragged the pail out. The bottom of the pail stuck and tipped the entire shelf of jars and jugs to the floor of the pantry. The clatter was fantastic but dulled by the walls of the closet. The shelf itself remained stuck to the pail. Lin lost hold and all that Dutchman's Gold fell to the floor. Honey oozed out thickly. She grimaced and turned her face away. Her gaze fell to the counter and the little honey bear container sitting next to the teapot.

"Of course," she said.

"What'd you do?" Jacy said.

"Shh, just making a mess and now we'll have to be doubly quiet. At least for a little bit." Lin fixed two mugs of tea with honey from the bear and brought them to the living room.

The honey on the kitchen floor kept moving, crawling only a touch faster than grass grew, but moving nonetheless. The kitchen floor dipped toward the stairs and the door.

George took a drink from his mug after sitting up. "Good."

"I kind of hope whoever owns this place doesn't come back. That honey's going to be impossible to clean up later, and I can't bring myself to clean it either," Lin said, coffee mug in her lap.

"Tonya, from school, her grandparents one time went on a vacation and came home to find a bear got inside and pretty much ruined the whole house. She said there was all this poop made of blackberries and stuff. The bear was gone by the time they got home, but that's how they knew for sure what it was, because of how the poop looked and how big it was," Jacy said. "Good thing we haven't seen any great big bears, huh?"

"Not long ago, there was a huge bear over the mountains, inland…you know what? No. I don't even want to think about what's out there," Lin said.

"So what do you think about because I keep thinking about what might be out there," Jacy said. "Then I wonder if there's something George hasn't seen in a comic and how big of trouble we'll be in then."

George had nothing to say to this, though blushed as he considered what Jacy had said.

"I'm thinking about my family. Have been non-stop," Lin said, staring vacantly at the TV.

"Your baby?" Jacy said.

Lin nodded and sipped.

"I never saw a monster moose in a comic…probably we better stay away from those," George said. "Just about everything else, but not mooses."

"Moose plural is moose," Lin said.

20

The remaining youngling moose had aged what would normally take a year in a single day and was rapidly approaching adulthood, despite that it had the life experiences of a newborn. The adult it had travelled with since its mother died giving birth was in the grocery store, exploring the bulk food section, stretching its long neck through the smashed front windows. The adolescent moose had eaten its fill and looked about the ravaged street. Curious and bored, it headed across the hard, hard road, clopping steps that echoed the entire length of the main street. A line of apricot trees separated a B&B from the sidewalk. They'd feasted much on the plums from the many trees around town—and everything else available—but the young moose wasn't on the hunt for fruit, and instead had an itch at the base of its neck.

Once bending its great head beneath the heavy shadows of an apricot tree, snapping many limbs in the process, the moose bobbed its head while pressing its neck to the tree. Previously unmolested apricots dropped from to the earth below, falling and rolling onto the street and into the grass of the lawn beyond the tree line.

By the time the itch was satiated, the twenty-foot tree was nearly bare on one side, stripped to the bark and then some in a few swatches that shined wetly beneath the pale moonlight. About twenty feet from where the moose stood was the two-story B&B. The building was taller than most on the block, slightly higher than anything within the moose's eye-level range.

On this roof, a massive cougar watched the unsuspecting moose. The cougar leaned its weight toward its hindlegs, the skin of its neck ruffling, its ears pinned back, and its claws out and piercing the warm shingles beneath it. It held its breath for a five count before leaping silently. It landed and the moose beneath it began rolling. Teeth tore and claws dug, removing the very spot that had been itchy only moments before. The moose let out an incredible distress honk.

The adult moose spun around, oatmeal dusted upon its entire snout. It broke into a sprint. The downed moose honked again. Blood poured from its wounds in a way that promised a short trip for the adolescent moose's lifeline.

The cougar only became aware of the larger moose when six points of its great rack slipped into its hide while eight more dipped beneath it. The moose jerked its downturned head back and flung the cougar high enough that it landed on the roof of an old school bus turned camper across the street. Two of the points had broken off an antler in the act, leaving behind small, jagged peaks. The cougar rolled from the top of the bus and fell to its feet and stumbled after a step.

The moose barreled toward the injured cougar and once again tilted its rack like the bucket of a skid-steer before jerking upward. The big cat cartwheeled, blood from its great claws raining out like sprinkler water. It did not land on its feet but did attempt to rise. The moose charged, getting to its hindlegs like a flustered horse before slamming the hooves of its forefeet down onto the once mighty lion.

The fight was over, but the beating continued. The moose slammed its hooves over and over, creating a fantastic puddle of blood that ran into the street, seeping into crooks and crannies, mingling with rainwater as if soaked into the soil and bedrock of Picture Island. That blood, like the blood of the space gator, was tainted with otherworldly DNA that adhered and transformed everywhere possible.

21

Mandy had closed her eyes for a moment, trying to regain her composure and if she were lucky, a bit of energy. She opened her eyes to six shining black heads surrounding her. As they had been before, they were of typical sea lion size, but no less scary way out there. An understanding flashed. She looked to the moon that was now shining brightly overhead. She had indeed fallen asleep. She jerked around, sending the seals underwater momentarily. The town was no longer behind her, not directly.

"Shit," she said, though was now closer to shore than she had been.

Trying to ignore the curious sea lions that watched her and the even more curious huge black blobs lying about the rocky shore beneath the thick forest, she pointed her back toward home and began kicking. Those blobs were intensely off-putting, and she wanted nothing to do with their attention. They looked how sea lions looked, glistening beneath moonlight, but all too big. It had to be possible that however the island was infected, it didn't touch every animal with the same strength.

"Say, you want to give me a ride in?" she said to a sea lion bobbing along next to her, watching her with its liquid black eyes.

The nap had increased her energy, but she knew it wouldn't last, not with how her guts grumbled. She thought when she got to land, and then to the hotel, that she might just drop a few hot dogs in the deep fryer. It was the most deadly yet delicious food she could fix, and she only allowed herself to partake once or twice a year. She'd last eaten a fried dog two nights after the gator business had ended.

"Earning them today," she whispered.

The ocean was calm, and the tide was headed in, though cutting north a bit and fighting against her effort to land near town, or preferably at the town's main pier. Two more sea lions reappeared near the first. They were eerily like domesticated animals, though she guessed if she'd slept longer, she might've become a meal.

"Survive a space gator, get eaten by regular degular Earth seals."

The trio of sea lions disappeared. Two seconds later, Mandy felt them, nosing at her. She gasped and stiffened everywhere but her feet. She continued kicking. She made fists of her hands and brought them out of the water. Nothing easy to bite. Her pent-up breath began to burn in her chest. She only exhaled when she noticed her butt rising and her speed increasing. The sea lions were helping her to shore.

They didn't acknowledge the angle she'd been headed, but that now hardly mattered. She was almost directly in-line with the buoy that had temporarily saved James South's life. If she got there, she could climb up, save up some energy, and give a good final push toward town through the shallows.

She thought this had to be a first, sea lions rescuing a human, but her mental database pinged a hit using the Mandoogle search bar. She had Twitter, just because, and scrolled irregularly, mostly to see what people were arguing about concerning *RuPaul's Drag Race* and to watch videos posted to The Dodo's page. One time they shared a story about a man attempting suicide down in San Francisco. He hadn't died when he hit, and surviving the fall left him tasting the full buffet of buyer's remorse. The water was freezing, and he was sinking fast. A sea lion had come along just in time to prop him up and keep him afloat.

"It's like you know I don't belong in the water," Mandy said, mostly to herself.

Within a minute, she had to begin kicking and patting. She rolled, trying to get clear of the helping noses. Once the sea lions took the hint, they bobbed back above water. They watched her kick. Mandy used her ears to guide her as the buoy created a subtly different splash than when the water rolled over itself. Within a minute, her shoulder struck the buoy. It took a bit of energy—energy she now felt she could burn—and got herself facing the ancient marker. After pulling herself around to face the ladder, she gave another look to the sea lions.

"Thanks," she said.

As she climbed out of the ocean, her imagination kicked in and she considered the possibility these animals were trying to feed her to something larger, perhaps something stuck on the beach. A seal or sea lion that had been infected by the alien DNA and wasn't taking it as well as many of the other animals.

At the top, Mandy snuggled in-between the rungs

and looked over her shoulder to the stony beach behind her. Somewhere near there, the space gator had first climbed onto the island, had gotten this godawful ball rolling. She saw nothing hungrily waiting on the beach and glanced westward again. All but one sea lion was gone. This final animal bobbed with seemingly endless interest.

"You let me know if that whale comes back, huh?" she said. "A couple good barks ought to do it."

22

Jacy had moved from the recliner to spoon against George on the couch. She was a bit broader than George, so his arm had to rise to fit around her. They were both asleep. Lin was on the second couch, dozing in and out. She had come to fully twice wondering where in the hell she was before memories flooded back like a dam burst. She'd cried quietly into the couch cushions, thinking mostly of Baby June. The third time she awoke, she was out of it enough to hear Chewy, the cat she'd had in grade school. It would be on the outside of a door and *skritch skritch skritch* and when Lin opened the door, the cat would take off. If she followed Chewy, the cat would lead her to the cupboard where the treats were kept. The cat would then look up at her with big sad eyes, begging for mercy upon a hungry tummy.

"Chewy, git," she mumbled a moment before realizing Chewy had died of a thyroid issue when Lin was in her third year of university.

Lin awoke some and looked over her shoulder. They'd killed all the lights but the one over the stove so that they might have some peace. Neither of the kids were moving around. The kitchen was as it had been, aside from the gallons of spilled honey…which now had strange tracks through the mess. Lin rolled from the couch.

Skritch skritch.

She stood in the middle of the living room, her shin bumping the coffee table after her first step toward the noise. She had to check the door to be certain nothing had come through. Once in the kitchen, she saw clearly that whatever had fussed about the honey, had come from and departed via the stairs. She kept her socked feet from touching the honey residue as she stepped down to the door. Locked. Lin frowned and peered into the gloom of the crawlspace. The gentle glow of pre-dawn shined enough light that Lin spotted a pull string switch dangling above the third stair into the squat area below the house.

Skritch skritch.

Lin paused, string in her hand. She listened. No sounds returned to her. She held her breath and tried to squint her ears to the silence, tried to detect what was there with a power she didn't actually possess.

She pulled the string and at least two bulbs lit. The honey tracks glistened on the stairs. At the bottom, next to the staircase, the floor of the crawlspace had been dug lower. Enough to provide about five and a half feet of headspace in front of a washer and dryer. Lin imagined the housewife of the old home crouching down here—given the amenities and decorative choices, she deduced the people who owned the place were old and followed the old gender roles.

"Maybe she was short," Lin whispered.

Skritch. Skritch.

Lin took another step down the sturdy stairs and crouched to see into the dim crawlspace. The far wall had a tunnel bore through. Dozens of gooey

remained along the bottom of the window.

Lin flung Jacy at George before bending to pick up one of the knives they'd taken from the Picture House Lodge. She waved it at the ants. If they understood what a knife was, they didn't care. The leader got close enough for the knife to slice through the ant's armor, but it kept coming. Suddenly Lin was beneath two huge beasts, golden honey and clear saliva oozing from their jerking pincers. Lin reared back and jammed her fist, and with it, the blade of the knife. The knife lodged and stuck within one of the ants' skulls.

Jacy was out the window when George spun. The only thing within reach was his mug of tea—the lavender flavor was gross, and he drank exactly one mouthful. Without a better option, he picked up the mug and fired it at the ants. The mug didn't break but the cold tea splashed against the ants. They instantly popped backward like a wave.

"What?" George said, pure confusion playing about his expression.

Lin didn't know, didn't have time to figure it out. Her shirt and pants were shredded. Her left forearm was sliced, though not deeply enough to bleed her out. She rolled to her knees and sprang to the window. She leapt through. George followed.

Skritch skritch.

Whatever it was about the tea that halted the ants, it was only temporary.

SKRITCHSKRITCHSKRITCH!

Lin got to her feet and looked around. Jacy wasn't with them.

"Where's Jacy?" George said.

An engine revved and a bleached pink Plymouth Neon cut through a wall of privacy fir trees. Jacy had eyes like saucers behind the wheel. The car was going about twenty-five when it nailed the house they'd only just climbed out of.

SKRITCHSKRITCHSKRITCH!

George bolted to the driver's door.

"Get in the back!" Lin said, trailing directly behind him until he detoured to the back door. She opened the driver's door. "Move over!"

Jacy didn't need to be told twice. She popped over the center console. Through the cracked windshield, they saw the ants parading out the broken window and the gentle steam rising on the cool morning air from a punctured radiator.

Lin pulled the shifter into reverse and floored it, aiming for tree limbs rather than trunks. The limbs *thwapt* at the windows in a chorus of one-handed claps, applauding their exit—or perhaps attempting to slap it to a halt. The tires burned at the dirt beneath them, the rubber scent big and bold, even in the car. They bounced over a curb and nailed the rear end of a large truck, pinching the Neon down beneath the bumper.

Lin put the car into drive. The front wheels spun. The burning rubber scent grew tenfold. Ants poured through the tree line and converged on the little car.

"Go! Go!" Jacy said.

"I'm trying!" Lin said.

"Go!" Jacy said again.

"We're stuck!" George said.

Within two seconds, ants covered the car. Their horrible pincer jaws snapping at windows and steel alike, though rocking the car and inadvertently freeing it. Suddenly the Neon was flying down the street and ants toppled free, launching like fast-food bags, slipping from car windows on a freeway. The final ant fell away a half-block before the engine barked, knocked, and started clunking.

"What's that?" Jacy said.

Before Lin could answer, the Neon stalled and they jerked to a stop. Lin put it into park and turned the key off.

"Just one thing. One damned working thing. Why can't something go right?" Lin said, yanking at the steering wheel, moving in time with her syllables.

George was turned around in the backseat. "The ants are gone."

23

Richter Cohagen stood in the lunchroom of his British Columbia facility. This one was secondary and had fewer bells and whistles, though to his surprise, had presented much more interesting returns. The giant she-bear they'd had under deep freeze, and were working toward cloning, was offering much more than expected by way of genetic reproductions. Though having a living breathing she-bear clone had as of yet evaded them, the contents within the she-bear's stomach and digestive tract gave them a bounty of plant life that had gown extinct eons prior to the dawn of man.

"And just where has Dr. Murdoch gone?" Cohagen said. He had a can of Red Bull in one hand and a half-eaten Alpha Man bar in the other.

There were two doctors and two mercenaries acting as personal bodyguards in the room with him. None of the others were eating or drinking. The two doctors were standing stiffly and speaking carefully.

"He's taking personal time…his physician called for—" Dr. Sheila Rodgers said.

"His psychiatrist also called us looking for him, but we're sure he's only taking a short leave," Dr. Godfrey Ho said.

Cohagen's eyebrows raised toward the top of his forehead and to a line of perfectly plugged hairs. "Oh?" He bit into the Alpha Man bar.

"He has a tumor, so he's having it taken care of," Ho said.

"Where?" Cohagen said around a mouthful of high-calorie, high-carb, high-protein bar.

"Vancouver, assumedly. Probably he got second opinions, which is why his doctor and—" Ho said.

"No, where's the tumor?" Cohagen said.

"Brain," Rodgers said.

Cohagen sighed after swallowing. "Those can take a while, huh? I'll have to hire a new scientist. I need a prehistoric she-bear."

"Right…we've made great—" Ho began.

"Can I see the latest failure?" Cohagen said.

Rodgers inhaled deeply before saying, "No. We incinerated it."

Quickly, Ho added, "It was hardly more than a small pool of liquid. We've already begun anew. We think we have the kinks ironed out. Would you care to see the plants?"

"There's nineteen species now. Outside us, you're the only man on Earth to have seen anything like them, and the only one to own any," Rodgers said.

They'd worked for Cohagen long enough to know that priority #1 was not results but was stroking the man's ego. Priority #2 was letting him think he was a genius while taking full credit for their work. Though the new priority #1 might've been to keep Cohagen from knowing Dr. Micah Murdoch had not only succeeded in cloning a prehistoric she-bear but had drugged and stolen the bear after a few acts of severe violence—assumedly brought on by the brain tumor.

Cohagen folded the wrapper from the bar into a neat square before retrieving his phone from his pocket. He checked the clock. "We're to be on the island by when?"

Ho waved him off. "There's plenty of time for a quick peek at our hard work…and the great success of Ricco."

"Take it as a sign of things to come in the very near future," Rodgers said, grinning, sweat trickling from her hairline.

Cohagen tossed the wrapper like a Ninja star at the garbage can across the room. It missed. Rodgers hurried over to pick it up and throw it out. For a few moments, the atmosphere in that lunchroom had gone cold and heavy.

"Lead the way to the flora," Cohagen said finally.

Ho gasped and grinned. "Yes, right. Follow us."

Rodgers was all smiles, even as Cohagen handed off his coffee mug for her to put somewhere. She hurried over to the sink, set it down, and trailed after the billionaire, her co-worker, and two scary dudes with very big guns hanging from straps.

24

It was a relief to Chuck when the mercenaries showed up, until Miriam pulled him aside and explained the facts of their being on the island, and that they'd watch any number of people die without qualm. Chuck sighed at this. He was dog tired and had assumed they could watch the door so he could catch some much-needed winks on a cot in the bunker.

"Oh, they might watch the door," Miriam said, "but not to benefit anyone aside from their boss."

"And who's that?" Chuck said.

"Can't say." Miriam shook her head slowly as she headed toward one of the unoccupied cots.

There were nineteen people now in the bunker and they could fit a few dozen more. Chuck guessed anyone who might come had already arrived. The sun was on its way up and through the night he'd watched things cross the parking lot that had no right to exist. Jumbo everything. The insects were probably the worst. As creepy and crawly as bugs were, the true nature of most of their features was so small that it went unnoticed. Big ass bugs had big ass features.

Chuck fixed himself a coffee. One man and one woman had brought .22 rifles with them, and aside from the mercenaries—who had pulled out huge automatic rifles after unloading filing cabinets that Miriam had quickly started fingering through—

those guns were their only real defense. Chuck still carried his Estwing. He'd cleaned the oversized otter blood away and the hammer went back to looking like it was meant for nothing beyond striking and pulling nails.

Most of the others remained sleeping and Chuck took his coffee upstairs, out of the bunker, to the lobby doors where he could look through and around the sheer curtains without drawing attention to himself. Scotty was there, standing at the ready for a fight.

"See anything interesting out there?" Chuck said.

Scotty pulled the sheer curtain aside some and pointed to an old Ford Festiva with a smashed windshield and a folded hood. "Moose stepped on that car."

Chuck huffed. Probably the damage was no worse than if the car had been moving and had struck a regular moose. Then again, little cars like that, if moving quickly enough, could get lucky and send a moose way, way over the car that the people inside got out alive. Thankfully, it appeared this particular Ford Festiva was empty. Chuck knew Roberta Watson's daughter owned the car. The daughter was only recently seventeen and had taken a job with the National Park. Chuck hoped she'd managed to get on the ferry.

"Strange we aren't getting radio signal, even from the ferry system. I kind of figured they'd be back already," Chuck said.

Scotty remained silent to this.

"You're in contact with the outside world. How is that possible?" Chuck said. "When everything else is down."

"Private network," Scotty said.

"And who owns this private network?"

Scotty glanced at Chuck with a look that said *Nice try, buddy*.

Chuck crossed the room and sat down. He set the hammer head on the floor, handle standing straight up next to his leg. He sipped from his coffee and tried to imagine what came next. He couldn't. He guessed someone with some firepower would have to come in to make it safe for them to live there. Miriam had asked him about selling and he told her that he hadn't planned on selling anything, though he understood that he might not have a choice. He might fight, or he might move to Florida or Arizona like every other old Canadian who was sick of cold weather.

"Where'd your buddy run off to?" Chuck asked after a couple minutes of near silence.

"Clearing for helicopters," Scotty said.

"Clearing what? The vehicles and whatnot?"

Scotty gave a partial nod.

Chuck squinted at this. "How's he going to do that?"

25

Mandy awoke shivering. The buoy was on a lean. The sun was on the cusp of rising, the sky a vibrant purple that slipped toward blue like one of those heat-detecting paintjobs. She stared vacantly, trying to calm her shaking body. The tide was out, meaning she'd have more mud walking than swimming in order to get back to the pier. Her arms were pained and numb, her back was stiff. She pulled herself up out of the ladder and looked to the beach. Silky black blobs lay about—nothing abnormal about that. She sat down, thought about something off about the shapes and looked again.

Those were otters, not seals, but they were the size of seals. Otters were sometimes playful, but oftentimes vicious and territorial. The last thing she wanted was to draw their attention—or the attention of anything else out there. As quickly as she could, she unbuckled the three hasps of her life jacket. The buoy was there so the hydro company could find its lines—they were buried once inland—and when they'd last been out to fix things, the team had left behind some garbage. Lucky for her—they hadn't been so lucky; they'd been ravaged at the hot springs by the gator.

She took a thick chunk of wire that had bent around the ladder and clamped her teeth on the cruddy green copper wire within. She tried her front teeth, and when that began to hurt, she put the salty copper end between molars. She pulled, hoping like hell she wouldn't lose any teeth doing this. Though losing teeth was decidedly better than losing her life.

An otter hissed at something on the beach. Mandy paused and watched over her shoulder. She was about thirty feet away and that felt too damned close. There was more hissing. She finally spotted the overlarge rat that had encroached on the otter territory. The group of otters had surrounded the rat, bolting in and out at the rat, hissing and shitting as they did so.

The voice in her head said, *Perfect cover if you can get your butt in gear.* She reefed and shook her head like a pit-bull on a Goodyear. The copper slipped a little, a little more, and then let go so quickly Mandy nearly lost the important piece. She let the copper wires fall from her mouth and tested the plastic tube. It was a hair smaller around than a take-out straw, but it would have to do.

On the beach, the otters continued harassing the rat, though had closed in tighter around it as a group. Mandy silently thanked the rat for its service, for its likely sacrifice, before she slipped off the buoy and into the ocean. The water came up to her knees at the moment. She stepped straight west until the water was up to her shoulders. She put the rubber wire cum breather tube in her mouth and began walking south. She had her eyes closed and was counting. She decided two hundred steps should take her past any trouble with the otters.

It wasn't as simple as she'd hoped and she struggled to keep from popping out of the ocean for a hearty mouthful, struggled against opening her eyes to inspect what had just touched her, struggled with the uneven floor beneath her. At least under the water, the gentle waves had little impact and weren't causing any further difficulty breathing from below. After what had already seemed an eternity of walking in slow motion, inhaling in sips and exhaling from the side of her mouth, Mandy reached a two hundred count in her head.

She stilled and slowly brought her eyes up above the surf. She'd been wading outward and almost gulped down water as a wave played against her nose. She took a long stride toward land and blinked away the saltwater—the ocean had always, always bothered her eyes. She heard the gentle clunking of the sailboats that remained tied to the dock. She also heard animals barking, but none were close, so she started straight in.

She scanned the beach. There was a large carcass of some sort, and she had a mind to skirt it when she got in closer. She now wished she still had the life jacket and could float out to the docks—the shore fell starkly away there, and she was too hungry to swim anymore without something holding her up. She continued the trudging steps, eyes darting around for anything untoward or overlarge. At least the weather was nice and the waters calm.

Quickly, she was up to her hips, then knees, and finally she was sloshing her heavy body through the mud. The mud shifted to slick rocks, slimy with seaweed and the usual skittering little bugs. The sandbank began then. Not nice vacation beach sand, but good thick sand, sharp with seashells and stones.

Something rustled ahead of her.

She paused thirty feet from the lip that went up to the forest, listening. She neither heard nor saw any further movement. She continued, angling toward the spot where civilization met forest at the edge of the ferry terminal's employee parking lot.

She got to about ten feet from asphalt when something rustled in the bush almost directly to her left. She held her breath and waited, waited, waited.

Nothing.

She continued, hurrying her steps. The parking lot ahead was almost vacant, vehicles dotting here and there like the teeth in a meth head's mouth. The nearest building was the ticket booth, which was attached to a small office. The window appeared to be open, even if the door wasn't.

"Fifty more steps," she whispered, playing the game she'd played out in the water.

It was then that she noticed she still carried the plastic piece of wire lining she'd breathed through. Something rustled behind her and rather than stopping, she broke into a sprint. She tossed the makeshift breather tube over her shoulder as if it might be a dog back there looking to play fetch.

Twenty steps.

Something slapped wetly against the asphalt.

Fifteen steps.

Mandy heard breathing next to her own and silently prayed it was an echo.

Ten steps.

Was that a growl? Had she heard a growl?

Five steps.

She didn't dare pause or look. She put a foot on a wooden parking chock that had been left beneath the open window of the ticket booth and launched herself up like a rookie gymnast giving a first try on the pommel horse. The bottom of the window hit her stomach and whooshed the air out of her, but she continued scrambling, shimmying, shaking, and jerking until she got herself up. Once her hips aligned, she tipped forward. Her pants caught and she dove straight out of them, or almost. They remained around her ankles, hanging her painfully over the desk. She whimpered and kicked. They rolled over her feet as she tumbled to the floor.

After a painful gasp, she kicked hard enough to detach her right foot from the pants, tearing them along an inseam from crotch to ankle. She spun to close the window behind her and paused. There was nothing out there. She began laughing and sobbing, her hand on the window. Nothing had chased—

A salamander the size of a Komodo dragon shimmied up the wall and popped its head in the window. Mandy slammed the window across, and the bright orange critter barely got out of the way in time.

She fell into the computer chair behind her and absently began unwinding her pants from where they'd been caught—on the corner of a boxy sound system mounted to the desk; the microphone with a bendable arm was wrench straight down. She took off her shoes and put her pants back on. The right leg flared out like the world's widest bellbottom when she stood.

The first thought she had as her heart rate slowed to normal was to stay put, but that wouldn't work. She needed food and a bed.

"Food," she said and as if acting as an echo, her guts grumbled.

Food might be doable. She opened the door that led into the office behind the ticket booth. There was a desk in one corner and a sink, mini-fridge, and a Formica table with two mismatched steel chairs. Above the fridge was a hanging cabinet with a faux wood finish. She bent to look in the fridge and found a sandwich she'd fixed herself in the Picture Lodge kitchen and had sold to whoever had been on-duty before life on the island spiraled to hell. Next to it was a liter bottle of water. Mandy snatched out both and dropped onto one of the chairs. She ate ravenously and drank so quickly she got three separate ice cream headaches.

Her stomach resumed rumbling, looking for more as she sat back, ready for a proper sleep. She needed to get back to the hotel. No sense sleeping on a floor when she had a whole ass hotel to sleep in.

She looked at the ruined pants, her skinny knee pointing out sharply, her leg in need of a shave. She almost laughed at that stupid thought. Who the hell cared about a hairy leg when there were real live fucking monsters roaming about? She then looked to the hanging cupboard.

Inside she found a cheap sewing kit in a plastic pencil case. Within it were needles, thread, pins, a stitch remover, a small pair of scissors, and seven safety pins. She dumped the case onto the table and retrieved the safety pins one at a time, putting her pantleg back together as she went.

Functionally whole, she stood and started toward the door at the rear of the office. Leaned up against the wall was an aluminum shovel. It had a square mouth and a stubby wooden handle. She grabbed it, took a deep, deep breath, and opened the door a crack. She listened and heard the loud rumble of heavy machinery. Within seconds, Buddy Hawerchuk's Caterpillar backhoe rolled by, though Buddy wasn't driving it. Dillon the mercenary was driving it.

"Huh," Mandy said and opened the door.

That engine would draw attention away from her. She hurried out, jogging with the shovel gripped like a baseball bat. Everything was quiet aside from the big yellow machine and it was all she thought about until she saw the smoke rising above the houses. She quickened into a run and got to the corner that would take her up to her hotel. Two blocks away at a straight shot, the smoke was thick and yellowy grey, likely from damp wood, or grease, or perhaps furniture.

"Huh," Mandy said, stopping her run and deflating.

The Picture House Lodge was a pile of rubble, still aflame, but obviously had gone up many hours earlier. From the direction of the hall, the backhoe's engine grumbled, and glass shattered before steel on steel made crunching car crash sounds. With nowhere else to be, Mandy followed the sounds to what seemed the only chance out of this mess. Though, what was life without the Picture House

Lodge?

26

"You hear that?" Lin said. She remained in the driver's seat, though they were sitting still.

The sound seemed to be coming from everywhere and Lin hit the power button on the stereo to be sure it was off. Heavy static poured through the speakers, and she hit it again to silence the sound. That other noise continued. The trio of heads craned on necks, looking through the back window.

"I feel it, too," Jacy said and then held a note to see if it vibrated audibly. "Uhhh." The vibration wasn't *that* heavy but was there.

"Think it's someone coming to save us?" George said.

Lin's eyes got wide and an image of Baby June flashed on her mind. She'd kept thoughts of death as far away as possible, and in the height of everything yesterday, it was easier then. There seemed to be more possibilities—natural assumptions about safety nets and emergency services. Now, though, the island seemed apt to crush them. She been through ghost towns before, abandoned homes, vacant buildings, and when towns go to ghost, animals creep in and take over. They'd had a night to creep in and roost in what appeared to be an all but empty town.

"Any weapons?" Lin said.

All looked around. Jacy came up from beneath

her seat with a telescopic snowbrush, complete with squeegee and scraper.

"Great, if there's a blizzard, we can clean off some windows," Lin said.

The back seat of the Festiva wasn't closed off from the tiny trunk space. George curled his upper body over the seat and reached down. He slunk himself back over, an aerosol can of compressed air in one hand and a jumbo bag of cat treats in the other.

"Nice choice of car, Jacy," Lin said, the sarcasm was gravy thick.

"It was closest and not locked and had its keys in it. My dad says people with cars like this want them to get stolen so insurance gives them more money than the car's worth after thieves destroy it. That's why I tried this one first," Jacy said.

It had gotten them out of the predicament with the ants, but now what? Did they sit there and wait, or did they follow the sound? As if in on Lin's thoughts, George spoke.

"I think we should make a run for it. If that sound is a helicopter or something, we don't want them to leave without us."

"All right, kids, bring your weapons and let's follow that noise." Lin kicked open the creaky door of the Festiva. The noise grew significantly louder, though really only seemed loud against the dead quiet of the town.

George had the compressed air and the cat treats with him. Jacy brought her snowbrush, stretching it to full length and twisting the plastic lock at its center once out of the car. Lin had only her fully developed brain as a weapon.

"Follow me and stay quiet," Lin whispered and headed toward a carport on the southside of the street they were on.

The bag shook in George's hand as he walked and seemingly out of nowhere, two rough looking, though completely regular, cats ran toward them. George slipped the can of compressed air into the crusty back pocket of his pants so that both of his hands were free. He opened the treat bag and dropped a handful onto the asphalt, barely losing a step. Jacy walked backwards, grimacing.

"Something's going to eat all the cats," she said. "I don't like that."

"Hopefully most owners took their cats with them onto the ferry," Lin said, unaware of what had happened to all the pets and pet minders who'd ridden the last ferry to ever depart Picture Island. She stepped to the driver's door of a Chevy Tahoe with rusty quarter panels and a cracked windshield. "Here goes," she said.

The door was locked. She tried the back door. She then hurried to the door into the home. All locked. She spun on her heels and was about to open her mouth when she saw the rat scurry out from beneath the truck, separating Lin from the kids. It looked left and right, hissing and turning to face Lin. It lowered onto its haunches as if to pounce.

George shook the cat treats. The rat spun quickly, smoothly, as if riding a turbo-charged lazy Susan. Lin bolted around the front of the truck and George dumped the bag, his free hand pushing Jacy back as he took a step in reverse. The rat hurried to the kibble, and once his beady little eyes left George and Jacy, they ran out to the street, Lin hot behind them.

"I should've hit it," Jacy said, lifting the snowbrush high. The telescopic shaft collapsed into itself despite that she'd locked it, arguing its futility as a weapon.

"How about we stick to—" Lin began but was silenced by a frog leaping into the street.

Jacy squeaked and swung the snowbrush like a baseball bat. The end pulled the telescopic shaft to full length and the stiff plastic edge of the squeegee lashed across the frog's face. A dribble of its lifeblood spotted, but that was it for damage.

"Uh oh," Jacy said.

The frog lashed out its tongue and snatched the snowbrush from her grip. It bent the elongated shaft once, twice, thrice, crumpling it before spitting it out. The noise from before grew a little louder and the frog hop-turned to face it.

"Run," Lin said.

The trio broke. Quickly the frog refocused and bounded behind them, moving just a hair faster than the kids. Lin led the way to the next carport. The vehicle was a Subaru and had a baby on board sign hanging by a suction cup in its rear window. She got to the driver's door and tried the handle. Unlocked, she fell in.

"Get in!" she yelled back over her shoulder, unaware that she'd outran the kids by about fifteen feet in a thirty-foot sprint.

Lin fell in behind the wheel and hit the unlock

button, just to be sure. Jacy and George both came to the passenger's side. Both piled into the back seat. George slammed the door just in time to feel the double thump of the frog slapping its tongue out before reeling its body against an unmovable object.

"Damn," Lin said as she felt the bare ignition.

Not six feet from the shotgun seat of the car was the door to the house. In the deadbolt lock, keys dangled. The frog scrambled onto the roof of the Subaru and all eyes went up. George had to lean into the middle seat as the tall can of compressed air was still in his back pocket.

"There's the keys," Lin said, more to herself than to the kids.

George followed to where she was looking and put his hand on the door handle.

"Don't!" Jacy said.

Lin turned back, wide eyed. "No—"

The frog flopped down onto the hood of the car. It lashed its tongue against the windshield. The trio gasped. A spiderweb of cracks paraded across their field of vision. George looked around the floor. He snatched up a Cabbage Patch Kid. It was dirty and battered. Without pause, he opened his door. The frog leapt back onto the roof. George flung the doll out behind the car. The frog chased it and George scrambled outside, his sneakers squeaking on the cement of the driveway. He made it three steps of four to the door when he flopped down.

"Close the door!" Lin shouted.

Jacy did, a steady moan in her throat.

The frog had latched its tongue on George's butt and was reeling him backward. George unbuttoned his jeans and wriggled. His pants began sliding down his narrow hips, revealing his now off-white undies beneath, before taking the undies along too. His ass cheeks were white, white in stark contrast to the shadowy carport and his semi-tanned legs—the touch of summer had almost faded from his flesh. He was almost to the frog's mouth when his shoes slipped off and his pants disappeared. In his socks, full moon rising, he broke for the door in a monkey run. The frog tongue lashed out, bypassing him and striking the door next to his face. George looked over his shoulder.

The frog was coming at him from about ten feet away. The tongue unstuck mid-flight and bumped the weighty animal heavily on the cement floor of the carport. Its expression seemed to change. Its belly began expanding, expanding, expanding. Its eyes bulged from their sockets. Its neck grew wider and wider and wider and then—*POP!* Frog guts sprayed all over the carport, painting George in gore.

"Yuck," Jacy said.

George grabbed the keys from the lock after spinning the deadbolt. He ran inside, hand over his genitals.

"What's he doing?" Lin said.

"He has to get pants," Jacy said, as if it was the most obvious thing in the world.

Thirty seconds after disappearing, George reappeared in a pair of too small Peppa Pig pajama pants. He was still barefoot. He headed for the shotgun seat of the car, stepping through the frog guts like they were hot coals.

"Nice buns," Lin said and then cackled madly.

George and Jacy looked at her like she was crazy.

And she was crazy, at least temporarily, a little bit anyway. She started the car and headed southbound. She stopped at a stop sign out of habit and the trio watched a moose as tall as a hydro pole step through backyards, heading in the same direction they'd planned to.

Lin looked at the fuel gauge, a quarter tank, and killed the engine. "Think we'll sit a minute."

"My dad saw a moose one time when he was driving. He said it didn't even flinch when he almost hit it. He said that's why you always watch for moose on the loose," Jacy said. "He says if you don't pay attention while driving when there's moose around, it's a big moose-stake."

Lin glanced in the rearview mirror.

"Oh *deer*," George said.

Jacy smiled widely.

Lin shook her head, couldn't help herself, and said, "You two are sure amoosing…going to die making moose puns." She began to cry with big wet sobs.

Jacy rubbed her shoulder and George studied his stolen pants.

27

The great moose had napped in a muddy clearing next to the road that led to the hot springs. It awoke with a sense of loneliness that was nearly as strong as its hair-triggered irritation. Since the change, every little thing felt like a slight that the moose needed to correct. Being alone only amplified the sensation. If it was to be alone, then so be it, but it would be solidly alone. It would master this territory and destroy any and all trespassers, big and small.

A noise rumbled distantly. This was something unnatural, from the place where the trees disappeared, and the boxy structures rose; where the ground stiffened, and everything stank.

The moose pushed to its feet. It stretched its spine. It had begun growing, slowly at first, before expanding to a height that made its fur ache—many animals in the huge forest on Picture Island had experienced the same growing pains. Now, it seemed, it was as big as it was going to get. Its fur was comfortable. Its rack was solid and heavy, even with a few points broken off.

That noise was big and grating. Head back, ears perked, the moose narrowed the sound's direction. It took a few steps, stopped a moment to sample the foliage at its knees, and then carried on to the gravel road—one that not many days ago, cocky locals had dragged a not-yet-dead space gator like a trophy.

There were other noises coming from those hard places surrounding the boxy structures. The moose ignored them. That big, big rumble was an issue worth dealing with—the moose would squash the dog before dealing with the fleas on the dog's back. Every other trouble could wait, the moose would get to it.

Through town, pausing twice to wince at the additional sounds coming from the direction of the rumble. Perhaps this thing would put up a fight. The moose resumed its slow walk, passing homes, vehicles, and oversized rodents without a thought.

Oh yes, the moose would get to all these troubles.

28

Dillon took his rifle and set out on foot. He wouldn't voice it, but he hoped to see more things to shoot. Moving targets were good targets. Life had gotten slow after his dishonorable discharge. He'd guessed he was lucky the pussy liberal critics and politicians didn't push for any further punishment than expulsion. They didn't see what he saw, what he and most of the good men in his troop knew: those people over there weren't even people. They were shaped like people, had flesh and blood like people, but they were not people. They did not value life. They sent children with bombs and planted landmines around hospitals. Thinking how they did, how could they be people? No, they were things to destroy, to conquer and mold—the white man's burden was to correct the world, shape it into a properly civilized place. These not-quite-people, out there in the sand, they were lesser beings.

And so what if he'd fucked a few of them and shot a few more? They didn't say the word 'no' and they didn't beg in any language he understood. By default, he would assume all wanted American occupation, all wanted to be conquered by the biggest and best. All those false gods were golden calves in the face of Jesus; calves were nothing but McBurgers awaiting their slaughter.

When he'd lost it all to the weak libs, he'd felt unmoored. He'd driven around Seattle, thinking about how many mosques and Islamic centers had popped up recently—his father had told him that back when he was a young man all those mosques were churches, back when America was great—and began envisioning a shopping cart rolling the aisles of Home Depot. He could get all the fixins he'd ever need to wipe the blights off the map. He'd learned things over there; they made bombs out of anything and everything out in the sand.

The call came before he even finished writing his shopping list. He'd been handpicked, and did he want to come down to California to interview for a job that paid more than the military, had better equipment, and maybe more importantly, his itchy hands would have something to do? Why, yes. He could focus on something other than the steady degradation of his country.

But it was almost entirely standing around and hitting the gym. If it weren't for the comradery—no racial quota needing to be met either—with his fellow former-soldiers, he might've stolen enough of Cohagen's equipment to blow away half the mosques in the country. Now though, on the island, he could shoot things—and one person. That hippy had held court in the lodge dining room and then again while camping on town property, declaring that nobody could own land, they could only rent it. When the action finally kicked in, Dillon had caught the hippy in his tent while the world scurried to the boat. He blew a gully through his skull with a 9mm Desert Eagle. He didn't even need to clean up the mess, strange grey globs had seemed to taste him through the soil. They rose and devoured the carcass. Dillon smiled, feeling better than he had in years.

Since arriving on the island some ten days ago, he had killed dozens of animals as well, one or two of them might've even posed a threat to him. Now, however, was not the time for fun. This was a period of focus. He'd noted the large backhoe one morning while on a walk, feigning the act of vacationing. He watched the owners of the home. One day they both left, and he entered the home. He located the keys to the backhoe and left them behind, untouched. Around town, he'd done the same with a John Deere Gator UTV, an F-450 with a wench, and a New Holland tractor, just in case. Cohagen had offered to send he and Scotty along with something bigger and more equipped than a Jeep Cherokee and a Dodge Durango, but Dillon had refused on the grounds of profile. Going unnoticed was important.

Now, he moved as he had in Afghanistan, cutting around buildings and dodging detection. He'd seen so many animals that exceeded their natural state. He wanted to kill them all; the sport of that made his hands tingle. First, though, he had to clear space for the helicopters and their payloads. There'd be at least five very large shipping containers to start, which meant he had to clear space for those and for at least two helicopters. Unbeknownst to most, Cohagen had already purchased the hall featuring the bunker. For image purposes, he and Scotty were to go along with suggestions made by some of the locals and those loading the ferry while actually leading the survival efforts along the way.

He reached the home with the Caterpillar backhoe unattested. He had to break a window to get inside, but there'd be nobody left to contest him. He carried a Heckler & Koch UMP .45, a canvas strap around his neck. The occupants had left, the neighbors had left, any nosey buggers across the street had left, so as he had last time, he entered this home and went about his business unattested. After retrieving the keys, he stopped by the fridge and grabbed a can of Caribou Lager, cracked it, and drained it at a go. He clenched his mouth into a smile after the final swallow and smashed the can against his forehead. Time to rock and fucking roll.

He climbed into the backhoe and started the engine. It rumbled loudly enough that Dillon understood he'd be drawing attention from animals and humans alike—though most of the humans had surely perished at sea.

He rolled through town at about 15MPH. The streets were clear enough that he didn't need to pause or create space for himself. It was almost a letdown. He'd been amped for the last forty or so hours and killing a few animals and one liberal hippy was hardly enough to satiate the hunger.

He reached the hall lot. It was relatively big, and only had a few vehicles parked there. Discussion in the bunker had concluded that these did not belong to locals, and the man named Chuck suggested the tour guides had people meet there to take vanloads around to see all the interesting locales. Dillon lowered the bucket beneath the nose of a Tesla parked in the middle of the lot. The owner had programed the alarm with audio from the classic film *Robocop*. "Dead or alive, you're coming with me," the heavy car said upon contact, repeating it. The backhoe chugged at the weight of the car but once it got going, it was going. The Tesla landed on its side, steel crunching, glass shattering, and Dillon began rolling, bucket against the car's undercarriage. It scratched violently against the pitted asphalt, still repeating over and over, "Dead or alive, you're coming with me," until it reached the edge of the lot. Dillon lifted the bucket again after positioning it just right and flipped the car down a gulley. The alarm ceased.

Dillon approached the next vehicle, an early '90's Thunderbird. He lifted the front end and the back wheels rolled cooperatively. The car picked up speed and dropped from the bucket, moving faster than the backhoe. The windshield smashed, but the Thunderbird rolled on. It hit the front of a split-level home and plowed through.

Dillon was then so focused on the front end of a Mitsubishi Outlander, that he didn't notice the people in the hall shouting and waving. Didn't see Scotty rush out into the lot and open fire. Didn't see the great big moose barreling down on him. He got the Mitsubishi's front end up. A regular alarm squawked irritatingly. He then flipped the SUV onto its roof and the alarm silenced. He noticed the rifle play in the comparative quiet.

The moose was not ten feet from him, charging with its rack down—not so differently from how Dillon had approached the cars with the backhoe bucket—at Scotty who was firing rounds at it. The moose was bloody but seemed unfazed. It scooped

Scotty and flung him backwards close to two hundred feet, sailing him over the rooftop of two tall homes. The man named Chuck was out there as well. He had one of the .22s from the bunker. The moose spun its head and whipped Chuck into a sideways barrel roll across the lot.

"Road rash," Dillon mumbled as he brought the HK UMP forward. He fired into the rump of the moose with a dozen clear shots before a hindleg lashed out, clearing the roll bars of the backhoe's cab and nailing him in the chest—like pounding him with a metal beach ball. He gasped and whooped.

The moose was bleeding all over and stumbling some. It still had enough energy to rear back and lift its forelegs. They slammed the cab of the backhoe, breaking the windows and short-circuiting the engine. Dillon had some of his wits about him and lifted the submachine gun. He let off several rounds into the moose's neck before the moose bent forward. The shots started breaking apart the great rack, but not fast enough.

The moose honked an incredible siren of rage and flipped the backhoe, losing more than half its rack in the process. Dillon spilled out a side window as the machine tipped—the seatbelt was coupled behind the seat uselessly. The roof landed on his hips. The HK UMP was in the cab, out of reach. The moose began battering the backhoe. The machine bled black hydraulic fluid and brown oil. Dillon wailed as he was ground into oblivion beneath the shifting backhoe.

The moose switched angles and stamp, stamp,

stamped, finally nailing Dillon's big square head, neck, and shoulder with a single shot. He was smooshed. The moose kept on stomping until shots rang out and stole its attention.

29

Mandy looked left and then right before crossing toward the Subaru. The din from the south end had the full attention of Lin, George, and Jacy. Mandy knocked on George's window and the trio jumped in their seats.

"Hi," Mandy said. "Glad to see you're not dead."

"Where'd you come from?" Lin said.

Mandy's clothes had waves of dried salt lines. Her hair was electrically frizzy. Her face seemed gaunt and droopy, eyes dark and puffy.

"Ocean—holy shit!" Mandy said, rising and looking down the street. She took five steps to her right for a better view.

Those in the car watched her watch the scene. Shooting had begun. Within seconds, something large and dark landed only a few yards from where Mandy stood. She disappeared from view of the car and returned moments later with a submachine gun in one hand and a fresh clip in the other. She squeezed the trigger at the ground and then jumped when three quick shots popped off. She ran to the car, Lin's side this time.

"Did you meet the mercenaries?" Mandy said.

Lin shook her head, mouth hanging slack-jawed, eyes hard on the weapon in the little woman's hands.

"There's at least two of them. They work for Richter Cohagen. He's buying the island, I guess.

My hotel burned down, so I guess that makes my decision a little easier," Mandy said.

"Sorry," Jacy said. "There were rats trying to get in the kitchen."

Mandy squinted, but let it go. "Anyway, one of the mercenaries just dropped out of the sky. He had this, though." Mandy looked at the black steel and figured out how to drop the clip from the weapon. She shrugged and popped the fresh clip in.

"Where do we go?" Lin said.

"There's a bunker. That's where I was headed, but the moose went there too…that'll be where Cohagen will come with back up. Probably we should head there," Mandy said.

"A bunker? Thank god. Get in, let's go," Lin said.

"Well, that moose that just went by, it's there, fighting cars," Mandy said. Suddenly the raucous din coming from that direction ceased.

"What?" Lin said.

"Guess I'd better go down there," Mandy said. "If that moose crushes the building above the bunker, it blocks the exit to the people in the bunker, probably. Think it was built for nuclear fallout, not explosions…or hoof-falls." Mandy straightened, tapped the roof of the car, and headed away. "Maybe you should follow me in case I need a getaway driver."

Lin did not move right away to start the engine.

"Go," George said. "You have to."

Lin made a face as if she was about to argue but sighed and turned the key. She put the car in drive and let it roll without touching the gas pedal after hooking a left turn and then veering hard to bypass Scotty's mangled corpse. Mandy walked along the line in the middle of the street and Lin stayed directly behind her. She had to brake before Mandy quit walking. The sight was too terrifying to absently follow. There were two bodies amid the mass of ruined steel and shattered glass. The moose had headbutted the glass from the front of the hall and had kneeled to shove its face into the space. Blood spots bloomed like dandelions on a lawn. Each had red, red trickles that oozed like vines. Blood was also leaking from its ears and playing tendrils from its mouth.

At the edge of the lot, Mandy crouched low. She aimed the HK UMP .45 and squeezed the trigger. The moose reared back, staggering sideways before locating the source of the gunplay. What remained of the beast's rack burst into bone confetti, and still, it kept coming. The spray swung in sloppy ovals as Mandy attempted to keep her aim true and failed, though most shots still hit the moose somewhere.

The moose thumped to ten feet away.

Mandy had to put both index fingers over the trigger to keep it pinned.

The moose was staggering, blood pouring from its mouth and eyes. It was now only five feet from the little woman with the powerful weapon. The submachine gun in Mandy's hands began to click, click, click and she tossed it into the damp grass where it sizzled with the heat of action. She spun and started running for the car.

The moose stomped behind her. It then coughed, spraying a hot, hot mist over Mandy before tipping and falling. It thumped lifelessly down on top of Mandy's small frame. Bones snapped, returning horrid echo cracks from every direction.

For a moment, nobody moved.

George was first. He kicked open his door and ran to the moose. He grabbed onto one of its huge ears and started pulling. "Help me!" he shouted, eyes frantic, expression pleading.

Lin got out and Jacy got out. A man ran from the ruined front of the hall. Distantly, two helicopters and a huge cargo plane approached.

30

Richter Cohagen arranged for the media to catch him in the act on the second day after he'd arrived on Picture Island. His crew ended up rescuing thirty-one people and were working on gathering up any pets not affected by the tainted water and soil on the island—and one animal that was affected; Chuck had bonded with a certain injured raccoon he'd patched up after he and the raccoon had battled it out with an overlarge otter.

Nobody asked concerning the fact Cohagen knew about certain things, and nobody accused his mercenaries of inaction, despite foreknowledge of activity in the ocean. Miriam Weever sent hundreds of emails and dozens of faxes; within a month, Cohagen would own the entire island, including the now former national park. He paid her handsomely. She'd signed away her right to speak of Picture Island, but when all land transfers were complete, she received the kind of bonus that let her retire early, should she want to. For now, she was going to take a vacation somewhere warm and landlocked.

Jacy's parents were off the cruise ship but stuck in a hotel for two weeks of mandatory quarantine. So, Jacy stayed with George in the hotel across the street from the hospital where Carole McNaughton had been transferred. Alexis and Carole's friend were also staying in the same hotel. Carole had tried to punish George over Zoom, but that wasn't easy as his celebrity had renewed and he had a steady stream of reporters and well-wishers telling him how great he was, though this time the hero was Mandy.

Mandy had a broken hip, a broken elbow, four broken ribs, and a punctured lung, but she was going to make it. Cohagen had purchased Picture House Lodge for more than double the value it had ever been because she was willing to sign a gag order concerning the damaging facts she knew about what went on involving Cohagen's mercenaries and Miriam. Mandy knew very little for sure and decided money was money, and in a world where money was worth more than lives, she'd better just take the check and ride off—once out of the hospital.

Lin got home and embraced her family. She got to work on the podcast, presenting every scathing fact she'd learned and every horror she'd experienced. In the end, it was eleven hours, and for at least four of those hours, it threw direct shade over Richter Cohagen. When the podcast aired, the CBC had condensed it and hired an unsuspecting radio host to walk listeners through a Ricco-friendly account of the events on Picture Island. Lin wanted to fight, but for now, she was home and that was enough to keep her plenty occupied.

For more of Eddie Generous' fiction, visit
www.jiffypopandhorror.com

Check out other great

Cryptid Novels!

Edward J. McFadden III

THE CRYPTID CLUB

When cryptozoologist Ash Cohn receives a gold embossed printed invitation inviting him to join The Cryptid Club, he sees the resolution to all his problems.Famous cryptid scientist and biologist, Lester Treemont, one of the world's richest men, and the leader of the Cryptid Club, is dying. What he offers via his invitation is a chance to succeed him. To take over his wealth, laboratory, and discoveries. All Ash has to do is beat eight others like him in a series of tests both mental and physical involving Treemont's collection of cryptids. Seems simple enough, and Ash has nothing to lose.Nine strangers from across the globe, all with reasons for wanting to win. When they start dying one by one, the competition shifts to one of survival. Who among them will rise to the top and reign over The Cryptid Club?

William Meikle

INFESTATION

It was supposed to be a simple mission. A suspected Russian spy boat is in trouble in Canadian waters. Investigate and report are the orders. But when Captain John Banks and his squad arrive, it is to find an empty vessel, and a scene of bloody mayhem. Soon they are in a fight for their lives, for there are things in the icy seas off Baffin Island, scuttling, hungry things with a taste for human flesh. They are swarming. And they are growing. "Scotland's best Horror writer" - Ginger Nuts of Horror "The premier storyteller of our time." - Famous Monsters of Filmland

Check out other great

Cryptid Novels!

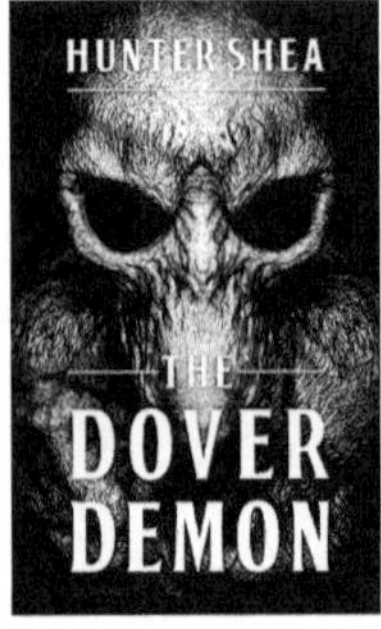

Hunter Shea

THE DOVER DEMON

The Dover Demon is real...and it has returned. In 1977, Sam Brogna and his friends came upon a terrifying, alien creature on a deserted country road. What they witnessed was so bizarre, so chilling, they swore their silence. But their lives were changed forever. Decades later, the town of Dover has been hit by a massive blizzard. Sam's son, Nicky, is drawn to search for the infamous cryptid, only to disappear into the bowels of a secret underground lair. The Dover Demon is far deadlier than anyone could have believed. And there are many of them. Can Sam and his reunited friends rescue Nicky and battle a race of creatures so powerful, so sinister, that history itself has been shaped by their secretive presence? "THE DOVER DEMON is Shea's most delightful and insidiously terrifying monster yet." – Shotgun Logic Reviews "An excellent horror novel and a strong standout in the UFO and cryptid subgenres." –Hellnotes "Non-stop action awaits those brave enough to dive into the small town of Dover, and if you're lucky, you won't see the Demon himself!" – The Scary Reviews PRAISE FOR SWAMP MONSTER MASSACRE "B-horror movie fans rejoice, Hunter Shea is here to bring you the ultimate tale of terror!" – Horror Novel Reviews "A nonstop thrill ride! I couldn't put this book down." – Cedar Hollow Horror Reviews

Armand Rosamilia

THE BEAST

The end of summer, 1986. With only a few days left until the new school year, twins Jeremy and Jack Schaffer are on very different paths. Jeremy is the geek, playing Dungeons & Dragons with friends Kathleen and Randy, while Jack is the jock, getting into trouble with his buddies. And then everything changes when neighbor Mister Higgins is killed by a wild animal in his yard. Was it a bear? There's something big lurking in the woods behind their New Jersey home. Will the police be able to solve the murder before more Middletown residents are ripped apart?

www.ingramcontent.com/pod-product-compliance
Lightning Source LLC
Chambersburg PA
CBHW051457050726
47593CB00005B/2118